TIME IS AN AMBUS

"Not since Graham Greene was creating his adventures has there been a writer with such haunting quality, the sweet sound of sad beauty which Clifford engenders ... All of Clifford belongs on the connoisseur's bookshelf; he is unparalleled in hovering suspense and distinguished style."

New York Herald Tribune

Francis Clifford was the pen-name of Arthur Leonard Bell Thompson (1917–1975), who was born in Bristol but pursued a career in the rice trade in China before joining the army, aged 22, on the outbreak of WWII. In 1942, as a Captain in the Burma Rifles commanding a company of Karens (native Burmese troops, he distinguished himself in the British retreat from Burma after the Japanese invasion, leading some sixty ill-equipped survivors on a 900-mile march through enemy occupied jungle and mountains to safety. He later served in the Special Operations Executive but turned to writing fiction in the 1950s, winning several awards from the Crime Writers' Association for his suspenseful and very humane thrillers. He later developed as a writer of spy fiction and one of his best-known books, **The Naked Runner** *(1966) was filmed starring Frank Sinatra.*

Top Notch Thrillers

Ostara Publishing's new imprint **Top Notch Thrillers** aims to revive Great British thrillers which do not deserve to be forgotten. Each title has been carefully selected not just for its plot or sense of adventure, but for the distinctiveness and sheer quality of its writing.

Other Top Notch Thrillers from Ostara Publishing:

Brian Callison **A Flock of Ships**
Adam Hall **The Ninth Directive**
Philip Purser **Night of Glass**
Geoffrey Rose **A Clear Road to Archangel**
George Sims **The Terrible Door**
Alan Williams **Snake Water**
Alan Williams **The Tale of the Lazy Dog**

Top Notch Thrillers

FRANCIS CLIFFORD

TIME IS AN AMBUSH

Ostara Publishing

Copyright © 1962 by Francis Clifford Productions Ltd

First printed 1962

A CIP reference is available from the British Library

Printed and Bound in the United Kingdom

ISBN 9781906288365

Ostara Publishing
13 King Coel Road
Colchester
CO3 9AG
www.ostarapublishing.co.uk

The Series Editor for Top Notch Thrillers is Mike Ripley,
author of the award-winning 'Angel' comic thrillers, co-
editor of the three *Fresh Blood* anthologies promoting new
British crime writing and, for ten years, the crime fiction
critic of the *Daily Telegraph.* He currently writes the 'Getting
Away With Murder' column for the e-zine *Shots* on
www.shotsmag.co.uk.

To
Peter Probyn

"Take what you want," said God. "Take it, and pay for it."

Spanish proverb

CHAPTER ONE

It had rained again during the night, as if from habit, but the morning was fine enough. Air and water were fused in the haze along the horizon; sea and sky two shades of the same soft blue. Once or twice during the past ten days the freak weather seemed to have spent itself. There had been other mornings of deceptive promise; brief, burning afternoons. Then the rain had come again, falling vertically from sullen, slow-moving clouds for hours on end. Even now there were a few dark strings of it showing against the blur where the sea and sky began, but the scarred peaks of the sierras behind the town were sharply defined and, without being weather-wise, I guessed that the worst was over.

For the time being the long crescent beach which curled towards Bandaques had lost its silver-white glitter. It was as drab as soaked coconut-matting, and for a hundred yards or so from the shore, beyond the line where the heavier waves started their final run, the sea was turning the colour of rust. Given an hour's sun the sand would bleach dry, but it would be days before the water cleared; weeks maybe. This was only the beginning. A vast mass of muck and rubble, borne on yesterday's flood from the shattered Lareo Dam, had smashed into the sea five miles to the south, and now the currents were at work, bringing the livid brown stain up past the promontory where the great tower of the Church of the Incarnation stood like a lighthouse, spreading it along the fringes of the beach far beyond the Villa Miramar. Already there were trails of debris lifting like dead fish on the crumbling waves and, inevitably, I wondered where Scheele's body was; and whether Ilsa had gone to her hotel window yet and seen what was happening. Only yesterday

7

afternoon she had said: "It's the first thing I do, Ty. I can see your house from there," though neither vanity nor hope could make me believe that would be her reason now.

It was warm on the terrace. For five months I had worked under the striped awning which slanted away from the wall facing the sea: a thousand words a day, five days a week. Weekends apart there had been no break in the routine until the morning Ilsa called to me from the beach—since when I hadn't written a single word. The typewriter cover was still on, and when I took it off and read the few lines on the page coiled in the machine they seemed stilted and unimportant; concerned people I'd almost forgotten. Recent events had made them remote and unreal and I recalled what Scheele had replied when Ilsa told him what I did: "I would have thought otherwise, Mister Tyler. I would have said you were a man who was interested in fact. Not make-believe. Real flesh and blood: real life and death. ... I am, Mister Tyler. There's no substitute for it."

It was still early; barely eight-thirty. Old Catalina, who cooked and cleaned and laundered, never came before eleven. I went into the kitchen and got the percolator started over a low gas, then ran a bath. As usual the taps, though boldly branded "Cataract", hissed and spat dementedly to no great effect, but I had long since perfected a schedule and was shaved by the time the bath was ready; dressing as the coffee came on the boil. Twenty-five minutes after leaving the terrace I was outside again, lighting my first cigarette, allowing the coffee to cool a little before sipping it.

Bandaques vibrated minutely in the returning heat, white and saffron and brown. For the most part it stood on slightly higher ground than the villa. On the promontory the buildings seemed to be all piled up on themselves, but as they scattered inland and along the coast they achieved a fairly uniform plane. There was a quarter of a mile of empty, dune-topped beach between the villa and the squalid outskirts of the town and it was still deserted except for the lonely figure of a civil guard. Every morning he trudged along the sand to a control-point three miles to the north, then retraced his steps into Bandaques. Another guard traipsed back and forth in the afternoon: yet another during the night. As an anti-smuggling patrol it was next to useless because I could almost set my watch by their bored comings and goings.

I checked the time now: nine o'clock exactly. The guard was a couple of hundred yards away, moving leisurely, looking curiously at the salt-laden waves. In the distance somebody opened a window in the Hotel España and the glass winked in the sun, catching my eyes. The España was Ilsa's hotel, a modern building with the shape and whiteness of a block of salt. It was half-way along the promontory, perched at the edge of a low, rocky bluff, and when sunlight was complemented by rain-washed air it was almost possible from the terrace to pick out the name emblazoned in gilt across the building's front, so close did it seem. Her room was on the third floor, the windows immediately above and to either side of the S, and I strained forward in an attempt to pin-point them, wondering again whether she was gazing out and seeing the after-effects of yesterday's disaster.

I had promised to call on her at ten-thirty. My parting words were: "I'll come earlier if you like. At any time. I'm here to help, Ilsa. Tell me what you want." To which she'd answered: "I want to sleep, Ty. Just to sleep. ..."

High and invisible, an aircraft was gently tearing the pale blue cloth of the sky. I drained the last of the coffee and stood up, an emptiness in me as I thought of her, a yearning that seemed to radiate outwards from some tiny and untraceable point within me. I lit another cigarette and started down the steps towards the crimson and purple flower-beds in the paved garden. Quite by chance I lifted my head for a moment, glancing along the beach. The civil guard was roughly where I had last seen him, except that he was now knee-deep in water, bent like a reaper as he struggled to get a grip on something close to his feet. I stopped to watch, imagining him to be after driftwood or some such prize.

A discoloured wave crunched in, practically knocking him off balance, and whatever it was he groped for was apparently sucked away from him on the backwash. He waded after it for a couple of paces, then turned about and staggered clear of the water, looking my way. Even then I hadn't really grasped what was happening. It was only when I saw him start urgently towards the villa that a slight chill went through me and I guessed what he must have found. And by that time I was running myself.

We stumbled towards one another, sinking through the sand's drying crust. I called: "Is it Scheele?" but the guard came on without answering, hampered by heavy boots and a slung rifle. When we were about twenty yards apart I called again: "Is it Scheele? The German?"—without realizing that he wouldn't know who Scheele was.

"A body ... in the water, señor." He was badly out of condition. "A man."

Stupidly, I said: "Is he dead?"

"Yes, señor." Halting, he sucked in air. "Dead. Very dead."

He started to explain about the backwash, but I cut him short. "Come on."

There was a froth of scum left by the tongues of failing waves, beyond which the sand was dark and soggy; shelving. A marbled rush of water whooshed in as we got there, breaking about our ankles.

"Where?"

The guard paused, uncertain for a moment, then pointed, and I saw something lift like a sack in the foaming shallows. Without speaking we waded towards it, growing less agile as the force of the waves increased and the backwash tugged at our legs. Twice we were almost within reach of the body, but each time it was snatched away. What looked like a jacket was twisted round the head and reddish water boiled furiously over the submerged trunk and rag-doll arms and legs.

Another wave crashed down. I managed to grasp an arm as the body floated level with me and tried not to think how

10

slimy it was; how alive it seemed. Blobs of spray stung my face. Half-kneeling, I yelled at the guard to get a grip on the other arm before the backwash set up its counter-pull. If he had had any sense he would have left his rifle behind. Now it slipped from his shoulder on its sling, knocking off his black patent-leather hat.

"Leave it," I bawled.

He lunged forward and made contact, nearly fell, then straightened up. The water sang as it slid back off the beach and what hung between us jerked like a puppet. We were no more than a dozen paces from dry land yet it took minutes to get there and all the time I was thinking: I'll have to look at him soon.

We dragged the body clear of the scum line. Without buoyancy it had become limp and heavy. I rolled it on to its back, then pulled the jacket away from the head. It was Scheele, all right, though the shock I felt was not because of recognition. From the first I hadn't expected it to be anyone else. But to bend close and see what had happened to him tightened my scalp and sent a flutter of nausea through me. Fear was frozen into the facial muscles. The thick lips were peeled back over the teeth; the blue eyes wider than I had ever seen them. Bright green weed was matted into his smarmed-down side hair and a single ribbon of it came from one clogged nostril. It was years since I had been involved with death, the first time in my life with drowning, and the ice-blue pallor of the skin sickened me. Even the freckles on the high bird's-egg dome of his head seemed to have dissolved.

I heard the guard grunt and say: "Blood." It was a relief to look away and I frowned up at him questioningly. "On the stomach, señor."

It was oozing thinly through the shirt: a fly had found it already. There was more coming from both knees which gleamed rawly through ripped trouser-legs. For some reason I hadn't expected a corpse to bleed.

"Rocks, probably," I heard myself say. "Rocks—and all the

battering he must have had before he even reached the sea. His temple's grazed, too." I stood up, noticing that one of Scheele's shoes had gone. "I'm going over to the house to get a blanket. Then perhaps you'll help me carry him."

The guard nodded. As I turned he asked: "Who was he, señor?" Before I could answer he went on: "Was he the man who was at Gondra?" and I said: "Yes. That's who he was."

I poured myself a brandy as soon as I got inside. When I came back the guard was standing in the water vainly looking for his hat. Scheele's dreadful fish-slab eyes seemed to stare at me as I spread the blanket out. I called to the guard and together we lifted him and covered him over.

"You take the legs," I said.

We had some difficulty getting him through the beach-gate into the garden: otherwise we managed without much trouble. But it was a slow business, for he was heavy, and I never once stopped thinking about Ilsa and how I should break the news. When we reached the living-room I was undecided where to lay the body. The guard suggested the window-seat, but because the blanket was sodden through I chose the floor. An odd gurgling sound came from Scheele as we put him down. It was unnerving, and the guard stepped back quickly.

I hadn't really observed him before. He was young, thickset, with a peasant's face. I gave him a brandy and took another myself. My hands were shaking. He emptied his glass in two gulps, then said: "I must telephone Captain Romero."

I lied to him. "Mine is out of order."

"Ayee." He clucked his tongue ruefully. "I will have to walk it then. ... Do you know the dead man's name?"

"Scheele. Erich Scheele."

He nodded. "The captain will ask." He seemed disconcerted by the loss of his hat; or perhaps it was inexperience. "On the other hand," he thought aloud, "I should remain with the body."

"I won't move it."

He hesitated. "And your name is—?"

"Stephen Tyler."

He repeated an approximation of it. "Thank you, señor." He stepped out on to the terrace, then came back, troubled by an afterthought. "You were acquainted with him?"

"Yes," I said.

"Then you have sadness." He glanced round the room as though he felt he ought to memorize a few details. *"Adios, señor."*

"Adios."

This time he went for good, jog-trotting along the beach. A more practical man would have used the road, but I had no intention of shouting after him to suggest it. Ilsa had to be the first to know: not some official. And I wanted to tell her myself.

My watch showed nine twenty-six. I went to the telephone and asked the operator to put me through to the Hotel España. Moments later they were connecting me with her room.

"Ilsa?"

There was no life in her voice and she sounded a long way off; her slight accent more marked.

"Can I come and see you now? I know I said half-past ten but I'd like to come right away. Are you up?"

"I am dressing."

"I could be there in five minutes."

She seemed to sense something. "What is it, Ty?"

"Can I come?" I insisted.

There was a short pause before she replied. "All right, then."

"Where will you be? Downstairs?"

"Here. ... The number is forty-two."

A pool of water was spreading over the tiles around Scheele's blanketed figure. As I shut the big windows which opened on to the terrace I could see the guard lumbering along the beach towards Bandaques. Then I walked quickly through the house and out to the convertible, glad of the air.

13

The Lareo Dam had broken at about four o'clock the previous afternoon. Some people in Bandaques were saying they had heard it go. It was possible, I suppose, though I didn't really think it likely because the dam was every bit of ten miles from the town, and barricaded off from it by a knobbly spur of hills. Others, with the wisdom of hindsight, were saying they had been expecting it to go for a long time. Already there was talk of a scandal over the maintenance contracts and there may well have been some truth in this.

It was a concrete dam: not large—three hundred feet or so wide—though large enough to carry a narrow road along the top of its high, curving wall. I had driven across it several times, usually of necessity, and had never thought it the safest place to be. Where the water poured over the swelling face of the dam from the spillway crest the concrete was patched and broken; and on the other side, when the level of the reservoir was low, the exposed area of sun-dried encrustation could be seen to be scribbled over with cracks. I once pointed them out to a man I met there, an official of some kind, who assured me with a shrug that they were only superficial. "If *you* were over forty years old, señor, and had had *your* face in water for a long time, wouldn't you show it just a little?"

I had smiled then, acknowledging my ignorance, but now, as I accelerated away from the villa, his words struck me as horribly applicable to Scheele. Yet it wasn't so much what immersion had done as the stark terror of his expression that haunted me: I imagined it must have formed in the very instant that he saw the huge, house-high torrent crashing down the empty valley towards him. And death must have come very quickly, fixing it long before the thundering head of water pistoned him into the sea below Bandaques.

For some time after it happened neither Ilsa nor I were aware that the dam had given way. It was only when we arrived back at the hotel and found the entrance lobby buzzing with talk that we heard the first garbled accounts. It would have been almost six-thirty by then, and another hour had elapsed before Scheele's continuing absence began

14

to niggle as possibly significant. We had sat in the American Bar and waited, expecting him to push through the glass doors at any minute; privately willing him to do so. *Where* had he said he was going? I couldn't remember and Ilsa had reminded me: "Gondra."

Gondra. That was it. Gondra. ...

A little later, provoked by Ilsa's increasing anxiety, I had asked the bar-tender where the place was. He was busy breaking ice and didn't glance up. "Gondra is about two kilometres down the valley from the dam, señor."

Ilsa's Spanish was limited, but she had caught the gist of it—helped, maybe, by the look on my face. "Where, Ty? Did he say near the dam?" And I, stunned, had been unable to soften the blow: "Below it."

Even then there had been hope. Scheele might not have been there at the vital time; could have been forced to make a wide detour to reach Bandaques. She had clung to every straw. And then, just on eight o'clock, Ilsa was paged. I had gone with her to the telephone, knowing that she would probably find herself in difficulties. Sure enough she very soon parted with the receiver, and it was to me that Captain Romero had introduced himself; explained that he was making inquiries about the owner of a cream-coloured Mercedes. They had found it near Gondra, overturned, embedded in red slush: and empty. ...

Much later, after I had eventually left Ilsa at the hotel and stopped off at Romero's office, he had given me the broader picture. Apart from some sardine boats swamped on the south beach and a missing herd of goats there was thought to be no other damage or loss of life. X million cubic feet of water had broken out and disfigured an already barren valley; crushed an already ruined village where no one lived or went. People were saying it was a miracle—as much a miracle as the dam was a scandal. But I was too tired and shaken, both then and on the final run home in the rain, to care about things like that; or to cope with all the questions that had besieged my mind.

She responded quickly to my ring. The door opened immediately and I could tell, as I fumbled for words, that she knew why I was there. Almost before I entered the room she said: "They've found Erich, haven't they?"

"Yes."

"Where?"

"On the north beach."

Her eyes moved to my legs and I suddenly realized that my trousers were wet from the knees down; caked with sand.

"You found him," she said almost accusingly. "It was you."

It wasn't a moment for splitting hairs. "Yes, Ilsa."

I told her about it as best I could. After a while she began to cry, quietly but without restraint. I gave her a handkerchief, damp from the sea. She sat on the edge of the bed and her grief swept me with a sort of despair.

Restlessly, I moved to the window. I had to go on talking. 'The guard wanted to phone Romero but I told him mine wasn't working. He decided to foot it. I suppose he'll have reported by now; there's no sign of him."

The long beach was shading from brown to yellow as it dried. The villa seemed closer than it really was and its pink, crenellated walls had the appearance of something made from icing sugar: it needed a conscious effort of the mind to accept that Scheele was lying there. Despite the remembered look and feel of him, despite the high view of the sea's telltale discoloration, an element of incredulity still had a foothold in my thoughts.

I turned away. Ilsa's eyes looked bruised, enormous in the smallness of her pale, oval face.

"Did you manage to sleep?"

She shrugged dismissively. I felt shut out and the silence became unbearable.

"I ought to go down to Romero myself. He'll want to know—"

She broke in: "How near the house was Erich?"

"A hundred yards or so."

For the first time in minutes she looked at me. "What ... what's he like, Ty?"

I should have known she would ask. There should have been a ready-made phrase on the tip of my tongue. Instead of which all I could say was: "All right."

Her eyes hadn't left mine. "All right," she repeated slowly. "*All right.* ... Oh, Ty—"

Her voice broke and she cried again. This time I went to her, held her, saying: "I'm sorry, Ilsa. God, I'm sorry." And though she clung to me I felt in my heart that anyone would have done in my place; another stranger like myself.

The telephone rang and she started. I released her and she walked round the bed. From where I was I could hear a man's voice and I guessed it to be Romero's. After a short while she began shaking her head. *"Momento, por favor. Señor Tyler. Señor Tyler. Si ... Momento."* With a gesture of defeat she pushed the receiver in my direction. "Please."

I took it from her: "Captain Romero? This is Stephen Tyler."

My being there obviously surprised him. He began: "One of my patrol guards has just come in from the north beach—"

"I know. I was about to get in touch with you."

"He tells me the body is that of Señor Scheele."

"That's correct."

"Where is it now?"

I thought it a stupid question and told him so. "At the house, of course."

"Alone?"

I closed my eyes. "Yes."

"You should not have left it, señor. Not unattended."

I heard another voice in the background and presumed the guard was saying something by way of self-justification.

"Look," I said. "I'm coming to see you. We both are. Can't all this wait until then?"

"How long will you be?"

"Ten, fifteen minutes."

"Make it less," he said with unexpected sharpness. "This is an urgent matter."

As the receiver went down, Ilsa asked: "What does he want?"

17

"To see us."

"When?"

"Now."

There was more than weariness in her sigh.

"It's inevitable, Ilsa," I said gently. "He's got a job to do," but I might have been talking to a statue. Once again I was filled with a sterile despondency. "Are you ready?"

She collected sun-glasses from the dressing-table and I followed her out to the lift. Nothing was said during the whining descent. As we crossed the lobby together the plump manager gave Ilsa an immaculate bow of sympathy and I was reminded of his words when bidding me good night eleven hours or so earlier—"A terrible tragedy, señor. I feel it almost personally. He was a most popular visitor here. Believe me, everyone is deeply shocked."

I screwed my eyes against the forecourt's dazzle. The heat was beginning to bounce off the tarmac and our shadows were as black as Indian ink. I glanced at Ilsa as I settled beside her in the car. Her lower lip was quivering but I could find nothing to say. We swung out from behind a pair of creaking manure-carts and headed along the promontory. The news-stands were doing a brisk trade in the morning editions and there were scores of people looking down at the sea over the pavement balustrade. I drove on—right past the fish market, left past the crumbling amphitheatre—and the nearer we got to the main square the more narrow and congested and noisy the streets became.

The Civil Guard building was a depressing, three-storeyed affair of grey cement and barred windows. As we reached it Ilsa broke our long silence. "What made him go there?" she said, in a sudden release of bewilderment. "What did he want to go to Gondra for?" It was a complaint rather than a question. Either way there was no answer and probably never would be. I waited a few seconds, then touched her arm. "Let's get this over."

The guard on the door eyed Ilsa with slovenly appreciation. Inside were peeling walls and a smell of must. There was a

18

wooden barrier some yards beyond the entrance and the duty sergeant took his time in allowing us through the pass-gate. When he did so we were led along an echoing corridor by a uniformed clerk who looked as though he'd slept in his clothes since their day of issue.

Captain Romero's office was at the very end of the corridor. It was a big room, larger by daylight than I had believed it to be when I was last there. A fan with only one surviving blade churned uselessly over the main desk, behind which, on a green wall, was a framed and flattering four-colour print of the Generalissimo. There were a few filing cabinets, a board full of keys, a smaller desk with a typewriter on it and a wooden bench set under the windows. The guard from the beach was sitting on the bench, still sweating from his exertions.

Romero rose to his feet as the clerk ushered us in. He was on the tall side, wide-shouldered, with a bullfighter's hips and neat, long-fingered hands. In contrast to the guard he was incredibly smart—the grey-green uniform newly pressed; his shoes shining like anthracite.

"Permit me again to offer my condolences, señora," he began gravely. "Perhaps there is some slight consolation in the fact that Señor Scheele's body has been found."

Ilsa nodded automatically and I didn't bother to translate. I envied Romero his formula. I said: "I suppose you'll want to go to the house?"

"In a minute or two. First I should like to have your version of what happened on the north beach this morning."

He was too officious for my liking. It had been the same last night, but I was beyond being irritated then. Now my nerves were on edge and his manner grated. I gestured towards the guard: "My version's the same as his. It's bound to be."

"Naturally. But I should like to hear it."

I snapped in English: "What bloody nonsense!" I gave it to him though. About six sentences were sufficient and I noticed that the clerk was taking them down. I finished.

"The facts aren't in dispute, surely? They're simple enough."

Romero shrugged. "It is merely for the record."

"Should I add what I had for breakfast? Which hand I shave with?"

His sallow face flushed. "I had thought better of you, Señor Tyler." He took his tricorn hat from the end of the desk. "All that remains now is for the señora to identify the dead man."

"Is that necessary?"

"Absolutely necessary."

"Despite my having done so?" I was thinking of Scheele's bared teeth and wide, terror-struck eyes; of the green weed trailing from one sand-blocked nostril. "Can't you spare her that? He's not very pretty."

"I don't lay the procedure down, señor. My duty is to see that it isn't ignored." He could be brusque when he chose. "Shall we go?"

We went with him to the street. The sergeant on the gate dragged his heels together as we passed. Romero's official car was waiting at the kerb. With bad grace I said: "There's room in the back of mine if you like."

He accepted the offer; squeezed his long legs in behind us. A blue-chinned corporal accompanied him. When we were clear of the worst of the traffic I spoke to Ilsa. "He expects you to make a formal identification. If you don't want to I'm sure I can talk him out of it." She stared straight ahead without answering: I was an intruder still. "What d'you say, Ilsa? ... You can refuse if you wish."

I shot her a sidelong glance. She was biting her lips in an effort to master emotion. After a few moments she muttered something I didn't quite catch. I leaned a little closer and it seemed to antagonize her because she turned her head with a fierceness that shamed me.

"I *want* to see him. ... I want to see him anyhow."

The town petered out amid patches of vegetation and leprous-looking rubble. The road ploughed a straight black furrow along the top of the dunes. To our right the waves appeared to be growing more and more sluggish as their colour deepened. Now and again I glimpsed Romero's face in the rear-view mirror—his brown eyes narrowed against the rushing air; fingers stroking his pencil-line moustache. It was only a matter of minutes to the villa. I turned the car into the gravel drive and we gritted to a standstill by the porch.

I led the way inside, then allowed Romero to go ahead. "Straight through." He entered the living-room. The sound of his shoes on the tiles stopped after a few paces. I heard his knee crack as he bent down. Ilsa shivered violently as we stood in the white, square hall and I could feel the goose-flesh on her upper arm.

"Would you come in, please?" Romero said quietly.

He was squatting by the body. The water had spread all over the place. Romero held one corner of the blanket in his fingers.

"A little closer if you would."

I continued to grip Ilsa's arm. It was like nearing a place of execution. Romero lifted the blanket.

"Do you recognize him, señora?"

She gave a small, choked cry. Time seemed to run to a stop. Scheele's terror had me mesmerized and all I could think was: That's long enough. *Long enough*—

"Yes?" Romero prompted expectantly, a vein branding his forehead as he looked up. "You know him?"

And Ilsa said: "He is my husband."

CHAPTER TWO

1

PRIDE and desire shrivel in the presence of death. But even then, behind the façade, they are at the mercy of a chance word, a secret glance, a casual gesture. One cannot hide from oneself for long. When Ilsa said "He is my husband" a part of me immediately countered: Was. *Was.* ... The guard on the beach had got the tense right: "Was he the man who was at Gondra?" And so had I: "Yes. That's who he was."

Was. *Was* my husband.

Romero let the blanket drop: stood up. He looked at me meaningly and I took his cue, muttering: "Let's go on to the terrace ... Ilsa?"

She was quite calm. Her face was like a mask and, when Romero opened the doors, she moved with me willingly. Under the awning was an upholstered cane seat where I sometimes threw myself when the writing went badly and I led her to it in preference to the hard chair by the typewriter. When I came back with a glass of brandy she was still bolt upright, sitting with the unnatural rigidity of someone about to be photographed.

"It would have been all over for him in a second, Ilsa. Try and hang on to that."

Her eyes closed behind the dark lenses and she nodded.

"Drink the brandy," I said.

"Can I have a cigarette?"

She had to steady it with her fingers before I could light it for her. "Thanks, Ty," she said huskily.

"Will you be all right for a minute or two? I want to speak to the captain."

She nodded again, but that was all. I went back into the room with Romero and we kept our voices down.

"What happens now? D'you remove the body?"

"Yes."

"There'll be an inquest?"

"A formality only."

"Will she have to attend?"

"No."

"When will it be?"

"Tomorrow." The slight lift of his shoulders indicated that this was only an opinion. Then he said: "She has taken it well," and you would have thought he believed that only the Spanish knew how to combine dignity with suffering. "Very well indeed."

Reflected sunlight shimmered on the ceiling. The rich scent of flowers and drying earth filled the room.

"My housekeeper will be here in about forty minutes," I said. "I'd rather she didn't arrive and find things the way they are now. How soon—?"

"The mortuary wagon is standing by in the town. If you would be good enough to drive me back to headquarters I can authorize its departure. Alternatively, I can start my corporal walking." He produced a wintry smile. "For the moment I'm in your hands."

"Why not telephone?"

"But yours is out of order."

"That's what I told your patrol guard."

"I see." He gave me a lengthy, quizzical look. "Well, that is the solution then."

I left him while he put in the call and returned to the terrace. Ilsa didn't seem to have moved: the cigarette had burned almost to her fingers. I took it from her and threw it away.

"We'll go back to the hotel when you're ready," I said. Then, carefully: "There's nothing more you can do here."

"Thank you."

"Is that what you want?—to go back there?"

"I suppose so."

"Another brandy?"

She shook her head.

"Romero's using the phone. As soon as he's ready we'll go."

He came through the door as I finished speaking. "Five minutes," he said cryptically. "Will that suit you?"

"Yes."

"I intend leaving my corporal here. Outside the house, naturally."

"Very well."

It was necessary to pass through the living-room to reach the car. Romero was not without feeling, for I noticed he had positioned a chair so that Scheele was partly obscured. But he needn't have bothered: I doubt if Ilsa glanced towards the humped blanket. She seemed to have shed her agony on the terrace. Outwardly she was taut and strained-looking, but she was more in control of herself than at any time that morning, and the part of my mind which had reacted against her use of the present tense had its say again. Even then, as the living-room door clicked behind me, I was able to think: She'll resign herself. A little while and Scheele will diminish. ...

The blue-chinned corporal was getting his instructions as Ilsa and I left the porch. Romero's manner worsened in the presence of his men: perhaps he felt a need to demonstrate his authority, but I didn't know him well enough to judge.

I drove slowly, disturbed by conflicting emotions. None of us spoke. The air pushed warm and gritty against our faces; toyed with Ilsa's straight fair hair. The high sierras were undergoing their first change of colour. They'd been blue two hours ago; now they were shading through mauve to brown. They made a fierce yet melancholy backcloth to the town.

The mortuary wagon passed us when we were about halfway to Bandaques. It was a closed truck, painted fawn, with nothing that I could see to distinguish it. Only the pressure of Romero's fingers against my shoulder told me what it was.

I dropped him outside his office. Ilsa's lack of Spanish was sometimes a blessing. I was able to say: "Will you want her any more?"

"I think not."

"If you should, I'd like to be present. Today, tomorrow—whenever it might be."

He gave me the same quizzical look as before. "I will try and remember, señor." Then, heels together, he saluted Ilsa. "Thank you for your co-operation, señora. You have been most helpful—and most brave. *Adios.*"

I drove round the square and returned to the hotel. It seemed a long time since Ilsa and I had been alone together. As we mounted the steps, I said: "What are you going to do?" It was no more than twenty to eleven. The day had somehow lost its shape. "You ought to eat. You haven't had anything yet."

"I couldn't."

"Coffee, then?"

We went into the American Bar and ordered. It was quite empty. We sat at a table in the corner under the mounted head of a bull which had killed four men in the Bandaques ring one September afternoon. A chromium plaque recorded their names and the date. There was no escape from the reality and permanence of death. The waiter who brought the coffee was grave and deferential: even his tired black tie had the stamp of mourning. When he had gone I lit a cigarette for Ilsa, then my own. Once more I was defeated by the futility of words and our exchanges were as brief as the tongue-tied silences were long. It was here, barely a week ago, that I had first met Scheele; here, last evening, that we had waited for him to return from Gondra. And now, though a fawn truck was jolting him towards the mortuary, his presence still lingered. I could hear his deep, mirthless laugh; remember his crushing handshake, the sensual lips, the glazed look in his eyes when he drank too much. ... It is ridiculous to be jealous of the dead, but the depth of Ilsa's grief was making it possible; and although I could tell myself that time would loosen his hold on her I already begrudged the waiting. Only yesterday I had said: "I love you, Ilsa."

After living blindly and intently for a long while a door had opened on another world with fierce and heady suddenness, and I wasn't able to slam it to as Ilsa had done.

In a fresh effort to break the silence, I repeated what Romero had told me about the inquest. I wanted her to need my help; to find me indispensable in the face of the various formalities inevitably awaiting her. Bandaques was a small town and did not, as far as I knew, offer much in the way of consular services.

"Have you thought beyond tomorrow?"

She moved her head slowly from side to side.

"You've got to be practical, Ilsa."

"You be practical. You be practical for me." She ground her cigarette in the bowl. "But don't let's talk about it now. Please, not now."

Chastened, I said: "I'm sorry."

She made a small, fluttering gesture of conciliation. Even so, her manner was detached and she didn't look at me. "I'm sorry, too, Ty. You've been very kind. Don't think I don't appreciate it. ... But everything's happened so quickly that I haven't really grasped it yet. I keep telling myself it's all some sort of dream."

"I know. I know."

"In the car just now I was thinking: I'll wake up soon. It can't be true. It *can't* be ... I really thought that. It was the same in the house when I saw Erich." She shuddered a sigh. "And again just now when you were speaking about tomorrow."

"I should have had more sense."

"Tomorrow can wait."

I said cautiously: "What about today, though? There's an awful lot of it left. How can I help, Ilsa?"

There was no reply. She had withdrawn from me again; gone into the dream. "If there's anything—"

"I'm going up to my room."

"Shall I come back later? In the afternoon, say?"

"This evening if you like." She tempered the qualification:

perhaps she sensed that it wounded. "Make it this evening, Ty."

"And there's nothing I can do meanwhile?"

"Nothing," she said wearily. "Nothing, thank you."

Minutes later I drove back to the Villa Miramar. It was well past eleven and for once Catalina had already gone to work on the living-room. The water was all mopped up, the chairs re-arranged, the used glasses removed to the kitchen, and for a moment I shared Ilsa's recurring sense of fantasy.

"Was anyone here when you arrived, Catalina?"

"No one, señor." Her face was as dark and lined as a bat's. If she wondered about the water she passed no comment on it. "Were you expecting to find somebody?"

"No," I said. "Not really."

I walked out on to the terrace and gazed at the white cube of the Hotel España. The strings of rain along the horizon had vanished and the sun blazed on the rust-red waves curling in towards the beach. This was where it had begun— less than a week ago. And I thought: God forbid that it ends here, too.

2

By eleven o'clock on that particular Thursday I had written a couple of hundred words or so; no more, certainly. They never come easily. Two days' torrential rain had temporarily driven me from the terrace, but the morning's fitful sunshine encouraged me to re-emerge. I preferred to work in the open and have the slow heave of the sea as an accompaniment to my thoughts. People who exist only in an author's imagination become no less real in his mind than those with whom he lives his natural life. While he is involved with them they imprint themselves over his vision and at times, while he strives to see them more clearly, his stare is oblivious of the existence of anyone other than them.

Vaguely I heard a voice call: "Señor, Señor," but not until the third or fourth time did it really penetrate my consciousness. She told me afterwards that I looked at her

27

for so long without showing any reaction that she thought I must be blind. "*Señor!*"

She was near the beach-gate, head and bare shoulders showing above the wall. I got up, a little startled. An arm appeared and she pointed towards the house. "*Por favor?*"

I gave her the benefit of the doubt and replied in Spanish. "By all means. Come on in."

Clearly, she hadn't understood. The dumbshow began again. "*Sí?*" she appealed. "*Sí?*"

"*Sí?*," I grinned, not playing fair now. "That's what I said. *Sí. Sí.*"

I remember, as she came through the gate, both my surprise and the thrill of pure pleasure that the sight of her gave me. She was wearing the briefest of bikinis and the tiny white triangles accentuated the deep tan of her body. She shut the gate carefully, then started up the steps between the flower-beds. She was slim, as small-breasted as a ballerina, and her hair was plastered about her head from swimming. In one hand she carried a schnorkel mask; flippers in the other.

"*Buenos dias*," I said, cheating still. "What's the trouble?"

The majority of good-looking women have an animal awareness of their physical attractiveness: this one had not. Her embarrassment was entirely due to her inability to communicate. Punctuated by sighs of exasperation she broke into another gesturing bout of mime. It was delightful to watch, but ungallant to let her go on.

"D'you happen to speak English?"

Her eyes widened with relief. "Yes, I do." Then she laughed. "Oh, thank heavens for that. I was making such a fool of myself."

"Far from it. But we weren't getting very far."

Beads of water sparkled on her skin. She had an almost boyish face, well-boned and symmetrical, with a generous mouth and wonderfully soft brown eyes. I imagined her to be in her late twenties—thirty, maybe; and guessed that her hair would dry out very fair.

I said: "It's a wonder the civil guard didn't pinch you."

"Pinch?" She frowned, and her literal interpretation went hand in hand with the slight accent. German? Swiss? Dutch, perhaps?

"Arrest you. Every Spaniard's a Moor at heart. He expects his women to be covered up."

"I know. I saw the notices." She had no inhibitions about my gaze; looked down at herself. "Perhaps that is why he took my clothes."

"The guard?"

"It must have been him. It's so ridiculous."

"Where were you at the time? In the water?"

She nodded, lifting the flippers and mask. "The only person in sight when I came out was the guard. I shouted at him but he was too far away and didn't hear."

"He couldn't have seen you either—while you were swimming, I mean. That's the only explanation."

"Then all I can say is he didn't look very hard." She was more amused than angry. "Why else would some shoes and a blouse and slacks be on the sand?"

Her shadow lay between us, fading as a cloud dragged over the sun. After all the rain there was a latent chill in the air.

"You'll get cold," I said. "Won't you come in?"

"I don't want to bother you. I was going to ask if your wife could lend me something to wear. When I saw the house—"

"I'm not married."

"Oh," she said. "Well—you, then. I can't go back to the hotel like this, can I?"

"Hardly," I smiled.

Had she been ten years or so younger I might have teased her in avuncular fashion: but I was too conscious of her body and the artless sophistication with which her eyes held mine. As she dropped her gear into a chair I noticed that the inside of one of her thighs was bruised and that she was wearing a wedding ring—discoveries which touched me with an absurd and fleeting envy.

I said: "Will you have a sherry while I look for something?"

29

"Thank you." She sat down, crossing her legs, pulling back a wet twist of hair. Completely at ease, she glanced round. "This is a lovely room."

"It's a lovely house altogether, but unfortunately I only rent it." I handed her the sherry. "If you busy yourself with that I'll see what I've got. Jeans and shirt?"

Alone in the bedroom I looked for them with fussy and unaccustomed eagerness. They didn't take much finding and, on my return, I displayed them like a draper. "What d'you think?"

"They're splendid."

"I don't know about that. We aren't exactly the same build, but they ought to do the trick." I placed them over the arm of her chair. Sunlight flooded the terrace again, shafting through the open windows, but her damp shoulders were mottled with cold. "There are clean towels in the bathroom if you want to dry off. Then I'll run you back in the car."

She protested, but I could tell she was grateful.

"And while we're about it we'll retrieve your things from the Civil Guard."

"You really shouldn't. I've caused you enough trouble as it is."

"It's no trouble."

She finished the sherry and stood up, absently brushing grains of sand from her stomach. More sand jarred from her ankles as she crossed the tiles. In the doorway she paused. "You know—when I called from the wall just now I was sure I was in for a dreadful time."

"How d'you mean?"

"I expected you to be an indignant Spaniard—all hands, eyes and moustache." She grinned extravagantly; struck an attitude. "With my vocabulary it could have been disastrous."

We both laughed. She was the most unexpected person.

"Are you English?" she asked.

"Yes."

"I thought so."

30

Presently, from the bedroom, she called: "What do you do?"

It was somehow flattering to be still in her thoughts. "I write."

"Write?"

"That's it."

"Books? For newspapers?"

"Novels and screen plays."

"It sounds most exciting."

"Far from it. It's a hermit's life."

I moved to the door and leaned against the jamb. Her voice shook a little and I supposed that she was rubbing herself down.

"And you live here always?"

"Oh no."

"Where, then?"

"All over the place. I've been here five months. In a month's time my lease is up and I go home."

"With a finished book?"

"I hope so."

There was silence for a while. I left the door and wandered out on to the terrace. Pewter-grey clouds were massing overhead. A small wind stirred, bringing with it the alien smell of a foreign land, reviving an old, inexpressible yearning.

"All those questions. You will think me very rude." She was behind me, clutching the top of the jeans into herself.

"Not at all." I watched her amused mock-pirouette. "A bit baggy here and there, but otherwise—"

"Baggy?"

A schoolday pun came to mind. "Toulon et Toulouse."

She frowned, baffled. "All right, though?"

"All right," I smiled. "Will you have another sherry?"

"Thank you, but I really shouldn't. I ought to go back. My husband will be wondering where I've got to."

"What's he been doing?"

"Sight-seeing. Wandering round the town. ... He is more enthusiastic even than an American."

31

"There's not much to see in Bandaques."

"You don't know my husband. Every brick, every stone—" She shrugged expressively, then gathered up the mask and flippers. "Did you really mean what you said about driving me back?"

"Of course." I stood aside to let her precede me into the hall. "Where are you staying?"

"At the España. We came the day before yesterday and it has rained ever since."

"The weather's gone haywire lately."

"Haywire?"

"Unpredictable—like my housekeeper. She should have been here at eleven."

"What is it now?"

"A quarter to twelve."

As I joined her in the car she asked: "Is she Spanish?"

"Who?"

"The woman who looks after you."

I nodded. "She is also very old and very ugly."

"I don't believe it."

"It's true," I said. "Regrettable, but true."

One ensnares the future in the gaiety of sudden escape from loneliness; unwittingly lays stepping stones towards some distant and unforeseen pain. At one time, if you had asked me where and how it all started, I would have answered: "When she called to me from the beach." Chronologically that was so. But every second offers a new beginning and now—much later—asked the same question, I would tell you that it was on the road into Bandaques, in the brief moment of banter when our eyes met and she chuckled: "You must be a very single-minded man." Something moved in me then and I sensed that she was aware of it—as surely as if her fingers had been on my wrist and felt my pulse quicken.

The grey-faced sergeant on duty at the headquarters of the Civil Guard was profusely apologetic; only too glad to part with the missing clothes. I imagine he'd already suspected that the patrol guard had been stupidly zealous and was relieved to have the evidence off the premises. The clothes were loosely tied with string. He wanted the owner to sign for them but when I explained that she wasn't adequately dressed to leave the car he accepted my signature instead.

I held the bundle aloft delightedly as I came out, then tossed it on to the back seat. "You were quick," she said.

"I gave them a piece of your mind."

I began honking my way through the noon-day traffic. When we were passing the amphitheatre she said: "Will you dine with us one evening? It would be ridiculous not to meet again."

"Indeed it would. I want my jeans and shirt back."

She caught my mood. "Then you will?"

"I should love to."

"Tonight, perhaps?"

"Tonight would be fine."

"I'd like you to meet my husband. He'll want to thank you, too."

"There's no need for thanks. Really there isn't. I've enjoyed every moment of this morning."

"Would seven o'clock suit you?"

"Perfectly." I was braking outside the hotel. "Here?"

"Yes. In the American Bar."

She extracted a pair of canvas sandals from the bundle of clothes and put them on before getting out of the car. I held the door for her.

"D'you know something? I don't even know your name."

"Ilsa Scheele," she said, holding everything precariously into her waist.

"Mine's Stephen Tyler."

She laughed infectiously. "I can't stop, Mister Tyler. And if I tried to shake hands I am sure those jeans of yours would fall down. ... Until seven, then?"

"Until seven. Good-bye."

I watched her hurry awkwardly up the steps. She didn't look back, but I drove home whistling.

Before seven o'clock came round I had opportunity enough to wonder what Scheele would be like. But he fitted none of my preconceived notions. To begin with I hadn't pictured so big and powerful a man. He was all of fifteen stone, though there was nothing flabby about him: his grip was as crushing as a vice. Heavy brows, pale blue eyes, hairy wrists, brown freckled hands, bald head—all these I noticed in the space of Ilsa's introduction. But what surprised me most was his age: as near as makes no difference he must have been fifty.

Weeks earlier, elsewhere, I overheard two waiters commenting upon a marked disparity in age between husband and wife. The younger one said: "I don't care to think of them together. It distresses me." When asked by his colleague why, if that were so, he continued to punish himself, he replied: "I can't help it. The state of my mind is the despair of a succession of priests." I had smirked with amusement at the time, but now, as I drew up a chair beside Ilsa, I experienced a pang of the same sort of sensual dismay.

Scheele was saying: "You did my wife a great service this morning. It could have been awkward for her if you hadn't come to her rescue."

His English was as good as hers but the accent was thicker; unmistakably German.

"It was my pleasure. I was under the impression that ladies in distress went out with the silent pictures. I'm grateful to your wife for disillusioning me."

I smiled at her. She was startlingly attractive. Her dark green dress was simply styled and her hair was short and fringed: except for the artificial redness of her lips, she wore no make-up. She looked very slight beside him; disturbingly fragile.

"Mister Tyler—" she began.

"My friends call me Ty." I was quick, too quick, perhaps.

"Ty?"

"That and no more."

"Ty is a writer, Erich. I told you, didn't I?"

Scheele nodded, big fingers wrapped around a sweating

glass of Scotch. He delivered his dictum about the relative merits of reality and make-believe, then added: "I imagine you know Spain well?"

"Not particularly."

"You have been here before?"

"Once—but not to Bandaques. I was near Malaga for a time some years ago." I accepted a cigarette from the proffered packet of Chesterfield. "Is this your first visit?"

"Yes," Scheele said. "We came by car."

"What made you pick on Bandaques?"

He shrugged. "I have business to attend to in Barcelona and thought this would be a suitable place for a few days' relaxation."

Ilsa explained: "Erich is a sales executive."

Scheele shifted his elbows on the table. "Typewriters." He mentioned a trade-name. "We're from Hamburg, Mister Tyler. One can have too much of cities. We wanted somewhere quiet—off the beaten track."

"Bandaques is certainly that."

Ilsa said: "The Tourist Office told us there is a fiesta on Sunday."

"That's so. It's the Feast of the *Virgen de la Tarde*. The Moors were driven from the town early in the twelfth century and legend has it that victory was due to the Virgin's miraculous intervention. I'm told they parade through the streets at dusk in her honour—generally cut loose with fireworks and so on."

"It sounds wonderful," Ilsa said with enthusiasm.

"Will you be here for it?"

Scheele answered. "We're staying about a week."

"If our belongings last that long." Ilsa smiled ruefully. "You'll begin to think we attract trouble, Mister Tyler—"

"Ty."

"I'm sorry. ... Ty." She leaned forward and I could see the shallow trough between her white, firm breasts. "This morning a guard took my clothes. This afternoon Erich had some things stolen from our bedroom."

"No!"

"I'm afraid so."

"That's bad," I said. "Were they valuable?"

Scheele said: "A watch, a cigarette lighter and a ring."

"While you were out?"

"No. That is what"—he searched for a word—"annoys me so much. Ilsa was sleeping: I was having a shower. It was after lunch—siesta time. I left them on a table between the two windows. When I finished my shower and came back into the bedroom they were missing."

"Have you reported it?"

"Naturally—to the manager and to the Civil Guard." His voice was suddenly charged with disdain. "But what can you expect? They are useless and inefficient and nothing will be done."

"That's a bit hard," I protested.

"I do not think so."

Ilsa sided with me. "At least give them a chance, Erich."

I said: "Generally they're the most honest of people. ... Isn't it possible there's been some mistake?—that you've mislaid these things?"

"Mistake? No." Scheele was adamant. "They were stolen."

"But how? Was your door ajar?"

"Ajar?"

"Open."

"It was not. And the veranda is separate from the others—you know, private. And the room is on the third floor." He drained his whisky; signalled for another. "Someone let themselves in with a key. There is no other explanation. But the manager defends his staff and the Civil Guard shake their lousy heads."

The theft dominated the conversation for some while. Ilsa endeavoured to make light of it, but Scheele's manner hardened the longer the matter was under discussion. I liked him less and lesss. He was a quick and heavy drinker and by the time we went in to dinner his mood had become one of contemptuous complaint concerning all things Spanish.

Ilsa eventually said something to him in German, and without understanding what it was I knew that she had delivered a reproof. He lapsed into a period of silence, but there was a continuing tension between them which seemed somehow to falsify Ilsa's attitude towards me. I began to have the feeling that she was using me; that her laughter was a shade too easily found, her interest in whatever I chanced to say a fraction too intense.

My conceit suffered. For a while I thought bitterly: Why fool yourself? You're a Boy Scout being patted on the back for having done the day's good deed—that's all. That's the only reason you're here. After tonight she'll have gone out of your life along with Herr Bloody Scheele and his surly manners and great enveloping hands. ... Yet not long afterwards, when I danced with her at the Bar Sinbad and Scheele was too fuddled, his bulk almost lost in the tobacco-smoke, for her to need to be anything but herself, I found that I was driven to say: "Am I going to see you again?"

"I hope so," she murmured. We were crushed together on the crowded floor and my lips were inches from hers. "I hope so, Ty"—and it was sufficient to relieve and excite my mind. We rejoined Scheele. For an hour or more we listened to the jazzy flamencos; watched the orgiastic expressions of the girl dancers. And all through the intricate rhythms struck by hands and guitars I was filled with a glow of anticipation that stemmed from the mood and isolation of our morning meeting at the Villa Miramar.

Scheele's speech had become slurred; his eyes slightly glazed. The theft had apparently ceased to concern him and he grew affably maudlin. Once he said meaninglessly: "They remember saints and visions because it doesn't hurt their pride. Otherwise they forget." And another time, leaning close, he muttered confidentially in his own tongue. I paid no heed: he could have said what he liked for all I cared so long as the whisky sapped his strength and arrogance. I was smugly content to suffer his arm round my shoulder and listen to his rambling, humourless anecdotes.

It was pouring rain when I took them back to the España. We had made our farewells and I was about to drive away when Ilsa emerged from the artificial brightness of the foyer. For half a moment I thought she might be going to ask: Where? When? But instead she thrust the borrowed jeans and shirt into my hands.

"Souvenir," she said gaily. That was all—but it satisfied; implied a secret shared.

3

Only last Thursday, less than a week ago. ...

The long afternoon dragged by. I picked at the meal Catalina had prepared; drank the best part of a bottle of wine. As usual she left soon after two o'clock. Had I not been going out that evening she would have returned at about five: as it was she had finished for the day.

I found the silent house unendurably lonely; the dull sound of the sea a constant mnemonic. For a while I either paced up and down like a caged animal or lay restlessly on the bed. The wine may have blunted my nerves a little but it had also plunged me into the blackest melancholy. Around four, on an impulse, I tried to telephone my agent in London in order that he should know that the novel was lousy and would be late. But there was a three-hour delay, so I cancelled the call. Later I wandered into the garden, plucking at the feathery tendrils of the pepper trees, mooching without admiration or delight between the scarlet flowers of the castor-oil plants and purple cascades of bougainvillea. Later still I took my shadow on to the dunes above the beach and, with my knees under my chin, watched the dung-beetles endlessly making tracks in the hot sand between the scattered clumps of marram-grass.

There was no purpose in anything I did except to kill time. It would have been about five-fifteen that I re-entered the house with the intention of having a bath. Hardly had I started it running than, above the hiss and belch of the taps, I heard a car crunch into the gravel drive. I went to the door immediately, only to have the sudden and unreasoning hope snatched away the moment I stepped on to the porch.

It was Romero. Disappointment must have filled my voice. "What on earth d'you want?"

"A talk with you, señor."

"Social or official?"

"Official."

"I'm going out in half an hour."

"Half an hour may be sufficient."

"It'll have to be."

He took my rudeness very coolly. "May I come in then?"

"If you insist."

He left his hat in the hall. There was a red weal round his forehead where the rim fitted. I turned the bath taps off before joining him in the living-room.

"What exactly's on your mind?"

"Señor Scheele," he said.

"I guessed that much."

"Guessed? Guessed what, señor?"

"That you hadn't come to talk about the weather."

He was moving around the room as if it were a shop—fingering a table, examining a lampshade—and I wished he would remain still.

"In a way you could say that it is about the weather."

I didn't understand.

"All the rain these last few days—the consequent strain on the Lareo Dam—the drowning of Señor Scheele." He seemed to think a picture needed straightening. "They are all stages in the same tragedy."

I still didn't understand. "Why's it suddenly necessary for you to speak in riddles? If you've anything important to say, then for God's sake say it. ... But hurry, please. I have to be in town by six."

He came to a halt by the terrace door, developing an apparent interest in something out at sea. "Would it surprise

39

you to know that Señor Scheele was not—as everyone has supposed—drowned?"

I snorted. "It would astonish me."

"In that case I should like to see your astonishment." He turned with theatrical effect. "The fact is that Señor Scheele was shot."

CHAPTER THREE

1

THERE was utter silence in the room. Outside, a seagull's cry pricked the soft thunder of a spent wave.

"*Shot?*"

Romero nodded.

"That's ridiculous."

"I'm afraid not." He was watching me, fingering his small, boomerang-shaped moustache. "A dead man cannot talk, Señor Tyler, but his body speaks for him."

I moved my hands in total disbelief. "But he was drowned. ... Drowned."

"No."

"There must be some mistake."

"A wound doesn't lie, señor. And there is a wound in his stomach."

My thoughts were going all ways at once. The seagull mewed once more and the thin thread was like a cry of pain. "I ... I don't believe it."

Romero moved from the door. "I'm sure it is difficult, but you will find that you have no choice."

I stared back at him.

He said: "Don't you remember the blood?"—he touched his abdomen—"the blood here?"

"Yes, but—"

"It came from a bullet wound. He wasn't drowned. He was dead before the dam broke."

"How d'you know that?"

"Because there is no water in his lungs. As I said, señor, a body tells the truth to anyone interested enough to look for it."

I ran a hand over my face; sat on the arm of a chair. Some seconds elapsed. "I'm sorry. ... It takes a bit of getting used to."

"That is only to be expected." His eyes hadn't left me.

"Have you been to the hotel?"

"Not yet. I only saw the autopsy report an hour ago."

Shock blunts the ability to reason. Automatically, I said: "Why've you come to me?—first?"

"Because you were a friend of the dead man. ... Because it is easier—since you speak Spanish—for me to talk with you than with his wife."

"He was hardly a friend," I objected. "An acquaintance."

"But you knew him."

"Only superficially." I quit the chair. "Anyhow, I don't see how I can help."

"That remains to be seen. Accidental drowning is one thing. But a shooting is a very different—"

"For God's sake!" I flared. "I'm not at school."

I brushed past him and stepped on to the terrace, angered by his pedantry, distracted by a dawning acceptance of the facts. The sight of the white cube of the Hotel España filled me with dismay. Telling Ilsa was going to be like saying that Scheele had died twice within twenty-four hours.

Romero joined me. "I'm sorry," I said again. "But the longer you remain with me the more you will have to endure my imperfections."

He shrugged. "You have been under a good deal of strain. I like to think, though, that you are going to be co-operative."

"In what way?"

"By answering my questions."

"I've got some myself."

"Such as?"

I turned my back on the sea and faced him. "Have you any idea who could have done it?"

"That is what I have to find out, señor."

"Or why?"

"No."

"There must have been a reason. People don't get shot without there being a reason." It had all come too fast for me. I was floundering. "Was he robbed?"

"No."

"How can you be sure?"

"There were notes worth over nine thousand pesetas in a wallet in his hip-pocket."

"He was robbed once before," I persisted.

"But not killed. This time he was killed but not robbed." I started to speak, but he went on: "Nine thousand pesetas is a considerable sum of money in a country like mine. Men work for a year for less. If robbery had been intended it would not have been ignored."

There was another silence as his logic sank in. Bewilderment made me restless. I walked back into the living-room and Romero followed me, as close as a shadow.

I said: "He was a stranger here. A tourist. Why should anyone want to shoot him?"

"With your help, Señor Tyler, I hope to come nearer to answering that."

"I've already told you—I barely knew him."

"You knew him better than anyone in Bandaques except his wife."

I felt his gaze boring into me again. I met it without caution. "Look," I said, breaking the pattern of the conversation, "I want her to hear about this from me. She's had a terrible twenty-four hours as it is. I'd rather tell her myself."

Romero touched his moustache as if to check that it was still there. "Is that where you were going at six o'clock?—to the hotel?"

"Yes."

"I think it would be wiser if you were to telephone to say that you will be late."

The sun-burst clock on the wall showed almost twenty to the hour. "What's going to delay me?"

"I am, Señor Tyler."

For the first time his tone bore a hint of menace and I reacted with some heat. "All I can tell you about Scheele will take five minutes. ... Less."

"That may be. But there are other questions I need to ask." He permitted himself half a smile. "Up to now, practically all the questioning has come from you."

"What other questions?"

"About yourself. ... About Señora Scheele."

"It sounds," I said acidly, "as if you have every intention of wasting as much time as you possibly can."

"When you are looking for something in the dark, señor, you grope. That's what I am doing—groping."

"I can think of other words for it."

He looked at me with disapproval, then subsided into one of two leather armchairs which faced each other across a low wrought-iron table. It was the act of a man embattled with authority. He extracted a cigarette from a metal case that came from his breast pocket, lit it with a match and blew a thin stream of smoke which deflected off the mosaic surface of the table and spread.

Against my will I conceded temporary defeat. I said: "How long's this going to take?"

He lifted his shoulders in the lazy, infuriating manner I was coming to know so well. "It depends."

"On what?"

"On you, señor."

"For God's sake—can't you give me some idea?"

He shook his head. "I'm sorry."

I wheeled away from him indignantly. The telephone was in a recess surrounded by bookshelves. As I reached it Romero said: "I would rather you did not mention what you know about Señor Scheele for the moment."

"You needn't worry." I was curt. "And don't spoon-feed me."

I could see the hotel through a window as I waited for Ilsa to be found. They tried her room first, then—getting no answer—arranged to page her. I suppose I had to wait a couple of minutes, but it seemed longer. The day was beginning to burn itself out behind the darkening sierras and a few pale lights were already showing in the hotel and elsewhere along the promontory. I practically forgot Romero's presence as the seconds passed. I was more conscious of a crude and burning resentment that the door which Ilsa seemed to have shut between us was now—through a twist of fate—going to be equipped with bolts and bars. Dismay was burrowing through me again, swamping my irritation, and with a sudden stab of hatred for Scheele I remember thinking quite without shame: Why couldn't you just have been drowned? Wasn't that enough? ...

"*Momento, señor,*" a woman said. Then Ilsa was on the line. "Ty?"

"I'm going to be a bit late, I'm afraid. I'm awfully sorry."

There was a momentary pause. "It doesn't matter."

"I can't say how long I'll be"—I glanced at Romero in appeal but he ignored me. To blazes with you, I thought—"but I shouldn't be later than seven."

"Seven?" She echoed it flatly.

"Yes. I'll explain when I see you." I asked her where I should find her; again apologized. "I wouldn't have had this happen for the world."

"It doesn't matter," she repeated, and her voice carried a hint of indifference which fed my longing with another dose of the same dull, jealous hurt that had been growing ever since we knew for sure that Scheele was dead.

I stared at the hotel for a second or two after ringing off, battered by a confusion of thought. Then I crossed to the centre of the room and sat in the chair opposite Romero. He stopped examining his long fingers and looked at me critically.

"Well?" His lips curled.

I lit a cigarette. "What d'you want to know?"

"Everything you can tell me."

"Starting where exactly?"

"At the beginning."

"Shouldn't someone take it down?" There was no one else

45

on whom to vent my mood and I had a strong desire to taunt him. "For the record? Or did your sergeant plant a microphone this morning?"

"Not this time," he said evenly.

"What sort of beginning d'you want? Mine? Where I was born? Who my parents were? Theirs? ... In which case we'll be here all night."

Romero uncrossed his legs; leaned towards me. I caught a faint whiff of garlic. "Let's not play games, Señor Tyler: you know very well what I'm after. I'm groping in the dark, remember? Very well, then. I'm simply asking for a day-by-day account of your association with Señor Scheele. Surely that isn't too much to expect of you?" He settled back in the chair, tapping the leather arm with a thumb. "A day-by-day account of your association with Señor Scheele ... and his wife."

His timing and inflection succeeded in squeezing a maximum of meaning into the apparent afterthought. I felt my face colour, but I was too tormented within myself to realize that his mind was already working towards what was, after all, an elementary conclusion.

2

I told him about the morning Ilsa had her clothes taken from the beach by the patrol guard; about the three of us dining together at the hotel and finishing up at the Bar Sinbad. I gave him the bare bones of it, without frills, deliberately abbreviating the account so as to emphasize my point that he was wasting his own time as well as mine. Somewhere a murderer was going begging.

Romero had a chess-player's concentration; a croupier's coldness. But he was more dogged than astute and was labouring beneath the icy exterior. I became aware of this almost immediately I had launched into my side of the story because he queried my statement about the guard having taken Ilsa's clothes. It was a completely unimportant detail, but since the incident had never been reported to him he spent precious time cross-questioning me before he seemed satisfied that I was telling the truth. Had my eyes not been on the clock I might have made more of it, but as it was I had no patience with him.

Eventually I protested: "What in the hell has it got to do with Scheele, anyhow?"

"I like to be methodical, Señor Tyler."

"Then all I can say is God help the drunk or the petty thief who finds himself in one of your cells. He's there for life."

He didn't rise to it. Very deliberately he drew on his cigarette. "This happened on Thursday, you say?"

"That's right. Last Thursday. A week ago tomorrow."

He nodded. "And then?"

"And then, what?"

"What happened after that?—after you drove Señor Scheele and his wife back to their hotel?"

"On Friday, d'you mean?"

"Friday, Saturday, Sunday ..." He flipped the days along with a motion of his hands. "You have scarcely started, señor."

The rain bucketed down until just before dawn on the Friday, and the sun didn't break through until after the nine o'clock guard had passed by. I was on the terrace by then, drinking black coffee and trying to will myself to start the day's work. I got as far as taking the cover off the typewriter, but that was the nearest I came to picking up the threads and immersing myself in an imagined situation. The sunshine wasn't going to last and I kept looking along the beach in the hope that Ilsa would appear before the rain set in again.

Despite the length of the beach the most popular stretch was below the promontory where there were umbrellas and fixed bamboo shades for hire and the odd gaseoza stall did business. Urban people talk wistfully of wanting to escape the crowd but they find the reality of isolation hard to bear, even for a short while. Only a comparatively few ever seemed to find their way along the dunes towards the villa—the more dedicated sun-worshippers, the lovers, an occasional family, the very shy.

And Ilsa. ...

I was somehow sure that she would come down for a swim, but almost an hour went to waste before I saw her. There was scarcely anyone about: even where they usually concentrated only a handful of diminutive figures was visible and I picked her out when she was still some distance off.

She was wearing a light-coloured sun-dress and was near enough to the water for me to guess that she was letting it ebb and flow around her ankles as she sauntered away from the town. I left the terrace with the alacrity of an autograph-hunter whose vigil had not been in vain and hurried through the beach-gate on to the shore, suddenly elated, striding eagerly over the dark, pock-marked sand. I waved once, but she didn't respond. Instead, deliberately perhaps, she stopped walking and turned seawards, shielding her eyes with a raised hand.

I had come quite close before she acknowledged me. She called a greeting, but her words were lost in the sucking hiss of the backwash. She was carrying her sandals and the hem of her dress was wet.

I grinned, and called back: "I thought you were saluting someone."

She splashed nearer. "Is that what it looked like? I was watching the gulls. They fly so close to the waves sometimes."

"They're hungry. You take risks when you're hungry. ... Aren't you swimming today?"

"I couldn't believe the sun would last long enough."

"You weren't far wrong." I frowned quickly at the sky. "The rains in Spain fall mainly on Bandaques: meanwhile, perverse world that it is, there's probably a heat-wave in Hamburg."

She smiled, tossing her hair. "And in London? ... Is it London?"

"Outside London," I said. "A place called Richmond. If I know anything it'll be raining there too."

We had started walking, slowly, without any destination. A pair of sand-martins sprinted away from us like clockwork toys: a scalloped tongue of water creamed in.

"You sound depressed."

"Englishmen invariably sound depressed when the weather's under discussion. But I'm not, believe me. Not now, anyway—though I would have been if I hadn't seen you." We moved on a little. "That's gospel truth," I said clumsily.

"Gospel?"

"Genuine. Honest ... I wanted to see you very much."

I was in momentary dread of her reply. Loneliness and life by proxy are dangerous training-grounds when desire suddenly excites the will: one can delude oneself, presume too much. If she had chosen to disarm me there and then I suppose I could have reverted to the role of Boy Scout without more than a mild bruising. But as it was she said nothing and her silence served as another stepping-stone towards wherever it was the next few days were heading.

Soft, invisible spray found our faces. We strolled with a sort of aimless intent. Presently she said: "Shouldn't you be working?"

"My publisher would think so. In any case, he certainly wouldn't approve of what I'm doing now."

"Relaxing?" She gave the word a delicious upward curl.

"Meeting a young woman without her husband's knowledge."

She pouted in a way that conveyed any number of things. "Erich isn't interested in swimming or the sea. This morning he wanted to go to a museum."

"At the cork factory?"

"I think it was there. Anyway," she said, "he wasn't able to go because there is something wrong with the car. He is busy with that instead."

Without warning, a flurry of rain spattered the sand. The

world seemed to shrink as the sun vanished behind a bruised, shifting fist of cloud. Instinctively, I gripped Ilsa's arm. "We'd better run for it."

It was seventy or eighty yards to the villa. By the time we reached the protection of the awning on the terrace the rain was slanting down in cords. We laughed together, a little out of breath, slapping our clothes.

"Is this where you write?"

I nodded. "And breed ulcers."

"It is difficult for you?"

"Sometimes it's difficult. At others it's just pure hell." I put the cover over the typewriter. "How about a sherry?—or is it too early?"

"Thank you."

I went inside and filled two glasses. When I returned she raised hers. "What do they say here?"

"Salud ... Salud y pesetas."

"Salud y pesetas." She savoured it, head cocked. "I can understand that. My Spanish must be improving."

She was enormously appealing when she smiled. Her proximity disturbed the senses. Physically, I knew all but her ultimate secrets: vividly remembered from the previous day the soft, tanned skin beneath the light blue linen dress and the lithe feel of her body when we danced. I was thirty-eight years old but my mind had the gauche uncertainty of twenty years earlier. I wanted to say: "You're very beautiful. I've never met anyone like you before." But the impulse died under the pressure of the reality of who she was, of Scheele's existence, and with a degree of calculation that surprised me, I thought: Wait.

I said instead: "Any news of your husband's stolen things?"

"Not yet." She drank, meeting my gaze. "I'm sorry about last night. He behaved very badly."

"He had reason to be annoyed." I was trying to be generous. "What with that and your car giving trouble he'll begin to hate this country."

"I think he does already."

50

Without surprise, I said: "Why?"

She hesitated fractionally before dismissing the question with a shrug. "Maybe it's the weather. ... Can you wonder? Just look at that rain."

It was drumming on the roof; flooding the terrace. The sea and the town were hidden from us. It was just past ten o'clock: Catalina wouldn't come until about eleven. For an hour or more—or until the rain lifted—we were totally isolated. All my inclinations were to snap the taut bonds of restraint: but I could not. Perhaps pride was at the root of it, but I waited to be sure—more sure than I was. She had given no sign of how her own mind was working; accepted our solitude with the same tantalizing unconcern with which she had brought her near-nakedness into the house. True, at the Bar Sinbad, when I'd asked her if I would see her again, she'd replied that she hoped so. And on the beach just now her silence had seemed to imply approval of what I'd said. But I could have misconstrued both the answer and the lack of one: misread what was no more than cautious tact. On the other hand I kept telling myself: She's here, isn't she? Why else should she have come to the beach and walked this way? ...

I showed her round the house. She was genuinely entranced by it. Twenty minutes or so passed and I let every opportunity go. We returned to the terrace and smoked another cigarette; drank another sherry. The rain was easing off and the sea showed with the vague mistiness of a Chinese water-colour but I doubted if we would see the sun again that day. I used the rain as an excuse to delay suggesting driving her back to the hotel, but in the end Catalina's arrival made the decision for me.

Ilsa grimaced. "I suppose I'd better go. ... Thank you for showing me your lovely house."

"I've enjoyed it." Catalina was clattering about in the kitchen. Now that our seclusion was at an end I was angry with myself. Ruefulness made me take the plunge. "Will you come again tomorrow?"

"Tomorrow?"

For a moment my heart sank: she sounded almost startled. "Tomorrow morning."

I could hardly bear her frank scrutiny. It seemed to go on and on. Then, with an unexpectedness that constricted my throat, she said: "It might still be raining."

"And if it isn't?"

"I should like to."

All at once my lips had found hers: clumsily, painfully. For a few seconds she yielded. A swift, wordless passion possessed us, compounded out of frustration and longing and uncertainty. Then, gently, she pushed me away.

We left the house like conspirators laden with surreptitious guilt. From the kitchen Catalina sang out *"Buenos dias, señor"* and I answered her with unnatural casualness. My thoughts were aflame with excitement and wonder. On the drive into Bandaques I reached for Ilsa's hand; received an answering pressure. But neither of us spoke. Already I was wishing the hours away that were about to divide us; becoming enviously distressed by thoughts of Scheele.

The cream Mercedes was parked some way along the street from the hotel as I drew up. If Ilsa hadn't been observant enough to notice it I daresay we might have sat together for a while and tried to find words with which to recapture and prolong the fierce moment of mutual discovery, then parted. As it was she pointed the car out. "He hasn't made it go." The disappointment in her voice echoed another relationship of which I had never been part. She clucked her tongue. Now he will be furious again."

The bonnet was open. Ostrich-like, a couple of men in stained overalls peered at the engine: Scheele wass there too, protected by an umbrella which bore the hotel's name.

"Shall I drive up?"

Ilsa nodded.

I went into low gear and crawled forward until we were alongside.

"What's the trouble?"

Scheele's glance took in the pair of us without surprise or suspicion. He was too resentful to be anything else.

"These men are fools," he announced. "Fools. They've been here over an hour and done nothing. They're monkeys, not mechanics." Ilsa and he shared a tart exchange in German: then he reverted to me. "If they can't do something tell them to find someone who can. I'm tired of making signs."

I might have been a servant. I opened my door and squeezed out into the drizzle. Scheele pushed the two men roughly aside to give me room. His bulk dwarfed the pair of them.

"We think it's the pump," the older one said in answer to my question.

"Can't you fix it?"

"Not here. The car will have to be taken in."

"For how long?"

"Perhaps a day." He was a mild little fellow, but he conveyed the impression that his patience had about run out. "We have tried to explain to the gentleman, but he does not understand. Again and again we have tried. It has been very difficult."

He had my sympathy. When I told Scheele he retorted: "Time means nothing to these people. A day could mean a week. They're unreliable." He wore his contempt like a uniform.

"Not if you keep after them." I broke off to speak to the mechanic again. "He can't swear to it but he's pretty sure it will be ready by tomorrow."

Ilsa said something and Scheele nodded.

I made a spur of the moment offer. "I'll take you to the museum, if that's what's bothering you."

Scheele grunted. "I'm thinking about Monday. I have to visit Barcelona."

The news lodged in my mind like a spark. "Monday's a long way off. How about this afternoon?"

"The museum?"

"Your wife told me you wanted to go. It's five or six miles. I'll willingly help you out."

Without noticeable enthusiasm, he said: "That's kind of you."

"Perhaps you'll both come?" I was as off-hand as possible.

"I don't know about my wife, but I would certainly appreciate it."

Ilsa was silent.

"About three?"

"Thank you."

He had mellowed a shade. At his request I instructed the mechanic to have the Mercedes towed away: stressed the urgency. Scheele invited me into the hotel for a drink, but I declined on the grounds of having work to do. It seemed best to go: I was too close to the moment in the villa to be able to trust myself. A glance could have betrayed us.

"Three o'clock, then?"

I drove off, leaving Ilsa on the steps with him under the umbrella. Her farewell was warily casual. I was torn between hoping that she would come to the museum with him and hoping that she would stay away. As it happened she chose not to come and I think she was wise, though when—just after three—I saw Scheele coming out of the hotel alone I experienced a dull stab of disappointment that was akin to physical pain.

The museum was within the precincts of the cork factory. Years ago, during excavations for an extension to the plant, an early-Christian burial ground had been unearthed together with numerous Roman antiquities. The company had erected a grandiose sandstone building which had become one of the main tourist attractions of the district, but – probably due to the rain – Scheele and I had the place to ourselves. A wizened old man in a moth-eaten beret showed us round. For an hour or more our footsteps echoed off the high ceiling as we moved about between funeral urns and sarcophagi and broken statues and numerous show-cases of pottery and verdigris-coated trinkets. I had seen them all before, but I was more uneasy than bored. My dislike for Scheele had entered another dimension—more intense, more subtle. I was learning that one can pity the cuckold and hate the deceit in the same breath as wanting to weaken his position, undermine his right.

Mostly he was silent while the guide chattered and I interpreted. He nodded from time to time; occasionally asked a question. Disparagement, I felt, was never far below the surface. It was nearly five before we left. The rain hadn't let up. I took him back to the hotel, accepted his thanks, once more refused a drink, then went on to the Bar Sinbad. As usual the waiter Joaquin was anxious to experiment with his English, but before long I returned to the villa and tried to kill the evening hours with a bottle of Fundador; willed the rain to stop before morning.

My version of this to Romero was severely curtailed; somewhat adapted. In point of fact all I said was: "Quite by chance I met Mrs. Scheele on the beach during the morning. It started to rain and we sheltered here—in the house—for a short while. She told me her husband's car had broken down, and when I drove her back into Bandaques I offered to take him to the museum at the cork factory in the afternoon. He was keen to go there. I picked him up after lunch and dropped him back at the hotel around five o'clock. I didn't see either of them again that day."

Romero listened intently, chin on hands. "Not at all?"

"Not at all."

"When did you see them next?"

"On Sunday."

"Not on the Saturday?"

"On Sunday." Spite made me add: "Shall I speak a little slower?" His jaw muscles bulged under the sallow skin: otherwise his self-control was complete.

Saturday had been the worst of days, the rain heavier and more continuous than ever, and I had known from early on that there wasn't the slightest possibility of Ilsa venturing on to the beach. All the morning I had mooched about the house, unable to work or read or concentrate in any way,

55

until frustration forced me into Bandaques. For more than an hour I had sat on a high stool at one end of the American Bar in the Hotel España, watching people come and go while I toyed with an air-mail edition of the previous day's *Daily Telegraph.* But neither she nor Scheele had put in an appearance. The bar-tender had had no knowledge of their whereabouts and I had curbed an impulse to have them paged: to inquire after Scheele's car was too flimsy a pretext, and it wasn't the weather for offering them the use of mine. For the same reason, when I returned in dejection to the villa, I had resisted a recurring temptation to phone. But I couldn't stay indoors for long: I felt imprisoned. Two or three times more before the day was done I had lingered over unwanted drinks in the hotel or at the Bar Sinbad. Once I had even cruised slowly about the desolate, rain-beaten streets in the vain hope of glimpsing them in a café or outside one of the shops that catered for tourists. But all to no avail. By nine o'clock I had become sullen and defeated as the day itself and had gone early to bed, filled with an aching intensity of longing for Ilsa that was in no way assuaged by the thought that on the Monday Scheele was going to Barcelona. Monday, on Saturday night, had seemed an unbearable distance away—as far-removed as our last brief, disturbing contact. ...

Romero flicked cigarette-ash from his black pistol-holder. He was as fastidious as a woman. "On Sunday, then," he prompted.

I dragged my thoughts back to where he wanted them. "We went to the bullfight together."

"By chance?"

"No. I called at their hotel and invited them."

"In the morning?"

"Yes," I said without patience. "In the morning."

I was watching the time. It seemed increasingly to me that this was a quite pointless questioning. Mostly, antagonized by Romero's manner, I was inclined to forget the supposed purpose of my recital. Now and again, in a renewed moment of near-disbelief, my mind fastened on to the fact that Scheele had been shot, murdered; and that before long Ilsa would have to learn of it too. At such moments Romero's questions struck me as all the more outrageously futile.

I went on: "The rain stopped at about half-past ten. I went to the España some time after eleven. The Scheeles were in the bar and asked me to join them."

(Nothing about the manner of our meeting, the disciplined thrill I experienced when I saw her, the way her eyes belied her careful greeting. ... Nothing about my saying casually: "What did you do with yourselves yesterday?" and the blunt, twisting pang that came when Scheele answered with a mirthless chuckle: "We spent it where days like that were made for—in bed.")

"He was complaining about his car not being ready. I drove him to the garage where he found that he was mistaken. We rejoined Mrs. Scheele at the hotel and it was then that I suggested going to the corrida."

Romero's dead stare relaxed momentarily. "You wasted your time. There are no bulls or men any more. ... I take it you stayed until the end?—saw the final farce?"

"Yes," I said. "It was a bad bill, I agree."

(Nothing about my not caring whether the fights were good or bad. ... Nothing about Scheele's almost mesmerized concentration, his grunted appreciation when a bull twice tumbled the scraggy, caparisoned horses, or the way in which sweat beaded his heavy neck and his lips tightened when, barely ten yards from where we sat, death waited on the tip of a poised sword. ... And nothing about the delicious agony of sitting thigh-by-thigh with Ilsa, bending close in order to explain what was happening—close enough sometimes for her hair to touch my cheek—and never once being able to speak one word of what trembled in my mind. ... These things were not Romero's concern.)

"And afterwards?" The question-mark was hung out like a baited hook.

"I reserved seats for the three of us for the evening's procession. They were in the tier on the east side of the Plaza Mayor." With malice, I said: "Under the plane tree with the Coca-Cola advertisement. I forget the exact numbers."

Romero produced another cigarette: it was a smuggled brand. "You saw the disturbance, then?"

I nodded. "We had a grandstand view."

The procession in honour of the *Virgen de la Tarde* had begun at nine o'clock. All day long frantic preparations had been under way from one end of the route to the other—tens of thousands of lights draped from tree to tree; garish, fragile-looking arches erected; tiers of seats scaffolded together at special vantage points and hundreds of benches placed end to end along the narrow pavement edges. A stranger passing through might well have thought that the frenzied activity was due to some impulsive overnight decision to honour the Virgin's favours on that particular day. Around eleven, when I had driven hopefully to the España, all was chaos. Every street looked as if the inhabitants had been in the process of fleeing the town in the face of an invader instead of arranging to celebrate the very opposite. Seven hours later, when we left the bullring, it had seemed impossible that the zigzag route could possibly be in readiness by the advertised time. Even at a quarter to nine, when we were struggling to our seats in the tier, a score of harassed men had still been hammering the outer shell into place.

And yet, astonishingly, the procession had started on the stroke of the hour. A horn blast from the far end of the square had brought silence slithering over the crowd like a dying leaf-rustle. For a short space of time Bandaques seemed to hold its breath. Then had sounded the muffled tap of a single drum and the head of the column emerged from the shadowy street which leads into the square from the precincts of the Church of the Incarnation. Behind the solitary drummer, at a slow march, had followed detachments of the armed services, followed in turn by a group of civic dignitaries. Then the priests had taken over, double files of swaying black and white figures, some chanting, some silent. Close in their rear had come a huge figure of the crucified Christ, borne aloft by many hands and surrounded by incense bearers, after which the first of the lay brotherhoods had made their way by in their coloured robes. Each member held a lighted taper and together they had presented a medieval spectacle, solemn and mysterious and awe-inspiring. The various brotherhoods were separated either by a phalanx of the Civil Guard or by another lone drummer or by emblazoned banners carried by youths dressed like pages. Eventually the huge sculptured Virgin, the miraculous one, had come into view. Mounted on an ornate platform which rested on the shoulders of numerous straining men she had lurched past our tier, complete with a gleaming halo of electric light bulbs, and all around us people had fallen to their knees and blessed themselves.

At a suitably discreet distance she had been followed in turn by penitents, hooded, masked, cloaked, some barefooted, others with their arms thrown painfully wide, some in chains, a few bearing heavy loads. Behind them again had come more brotherhoods, more detachments of soldiers, more dignitaries, more priests, and—finally—bringing up the rear, a bishop busily distributing his blessing to the accompaniment of restrained music from a brass band.

It had made an impressive hour and a quarter; impressive enough to ease the tension of the charade that, since morning, Scheele's proximity had forced upon Ilsa and me. His presence had fostered my natural distaste for him, and it was a relief to be distracted. Ilsa and I scarcely spoke, though a glance can convey more than a spate of words. The parade had had a magnetic quality and the only time our attentions were seriously diverted was immediately after the Virgin had jolted past. Suddenly there was a shout; a scuffle. A man—it happened too quickly for any of us to be sure whether he was participant or onlooker—had dodged through the moving columns, pursued by a couple of Civil Guards who lined the route. For half a minute or so there had been pandemonium as hunters and hunted thrashed their way through the watching crowds. There was a tumult of boos and laughter, gradually drowned by indignant hisses. The chase eventually passed from our field of vision, but after silence had settled over us again I well recall Scheele leaning forward and—across Ilsa—saying to me with heavy humour: "I wonder if that's the fellow who broke into our room?"

The memory made me ask: "Did you catch him?" I leaned back and clicked on a light.

Romero shook his head. "No one has ever caught Zavella." Perhaps my surprise at the name showed itself. "You know of him, of course?"

"No." It was best to lie, if only to prevent more wasted minutes. Already we'd been an hour together.

"I thought everyone in these parts knew of Luis Zavella."

"You must complete my education some time."

There was an arid pause, during which, once again, the incredible thought came to me that, while we talked, Scheele's body was stiffening in a refrigerated cabinet in the mortuary with a bullet-wound in the stomach.

Romero lightly tested the proof of his moustache. "On Sunday, then, Señor Tyler, you were with the Scheeles for most of the day?"

"I've just told you that."

"And on the Monday were you also with them for most of the day?"

"No," I said. "Scheele went to Barcelona on Monday."

"Alone?"

"I believe so. It was a business trip. His business—not mine," I added pointedly.

"What did *you* do?"

"I don't see how that's relevant—no matter how much you say you're groping."

"No?"

"No, I don't."

Again the measured shrug. "At what time did he return from Barcelona?"

"About eight, I believe."

"You saw him?"

"We met at the Bar Sinbad." I anticipated his follow-up. "Quite by chance."

"Together with his wife?"

(Somewhere deep in my mind the correction insisted: Widow.) "She was there, yes."

"How had she spent the day?—during her husband's absence."

I shifted in my seat; felt a slow flush colour my face again. "That's not relevant either."

"You don't know?"

"Good God," I snapped. "What *is* this?"

"Just another question, señor."

"Well, I don't answer that sort of question."

Smoke wandered from Romero's mouth across his narrowed eyes. Unblinking, they never budged from mine. I suppose I should have realized by then what was coming but I was still blind to it.

"I won't press you," Romero said. "I hoped, though, that you would co-operate as much as possible."

"I have. But once you become unreasonable I shut up like a clam. And the line you're taking *is* unreasonable. More— it's damned impertinent." I smashed out my cigarette in the tray; glanced at the clock. "There's nothing more I can usefully tell you. I didn't see Scheele again after we met at the Bar Sinbad on Monday night—not alive, that is."

"No?"

"No," I said angrily. "D'you want it in writing or something?" I stood up, intending the move as a gesture of dismissal. "Now, if you'll excuse me–"

Romero stayed where he was. "There is one more thing, Señor Tyler."

"What?"

"Yesterday ... Tuesday." He waited.

"Yes?"

"Where were you?"

"Where was *I*?"

"What were you doing? Who were you with? Where did you go? ... In other words, señor, I should like you to account for your own movements between dawn and the time I spoke to you on the telephone at the Hotel España to report that a Mercedes saloon had been found wrecked below Gondra."

I was dumbfounded

"And on this occasion," Romero said, his voice gritty with revived menace, "it would be better if you chose to reply."

Eventually, when the initial turmoil of amazement subsided, I think I said: "Have you gone absolutely mad?"

He didn't react.

"Are you implying that you suspect I had something to do with Scheele's death?"

"I am asking you to account for your movements at the material time, that is all."

"It amounts to the same thing." I snorted indignantly; laughed. "If it weren't so absurd I should enjoy this. My God! And to think that for the last hour or so—"

"Where were you yesterday, Señor Tyler?"

With deliberation I took a cigarette from the box on the table in front of him and lit it; tossed the match down. "I suggest you find out. And then I suggest that you come back here and apologize."

His eyes flashed. "I will apologize to no one about this matter. Least of all to you, señor."

"Perhaps you'll resign instead." I blew smoke. "What you're suggesting is too ridiculous for words."

"It is for you to prove it so."

"You haven't got me in a cellar with lights on my face yet."

"That can be arranged, if necessary. This is a small town, señor, and what happens here is my affair."

He glared at me. In the long pause that followed I heard the dull sound of the surf again. It was nearly dark outside: a bat flitted past the window.

"Tell me this," I said, rashly now, and with scorn. "Why should *I* kill Scheele? There are perhaps two thousand people in and around Bandaques. Why, with your second-hand omniscience, d'you pick on me?"

"I have picked on no one. I have merely asked you a particular question."

"Why?"

He took his time. "You yourself said earlier that people don't usually get shot without there being a reason."

"Agreed."

"Very well, then. ... There may be two thousand people in and around Bandaques, Señor Tyler, but I suggest that you are the only one who is personally interested in the dead man's wife."

CHAPTER FOUR

1

My voice, when it came, had no edge to it; only a sort of weary exasperation. "You should have been a priest, capitán."

"I considered it once." Now that he was more in control of himself and had regained the initiative Romero allowed himself another of his rare half smiles. "The Church is in error, señor. Priests should marry, then they would have a closer understanding of the world."

"Yours, to say the least, strikes me as warped and naïve."

He rode it smoothly. "You are entitled to your views. My sole interest is in where you were at certain times: what you did. If my request is as preposterous as you make out, you have a very simple remedy."

I turned abruptly away from him and poured myself a brandy.

"Answer me," Romero said to my back. "Have you got a gun?"

"No."

"Have you ever had one?"

"When I was about six. It fired a bit of cork on the end of a piece of string. I killed my parents with it almost daily."

He was icy. "A real gun."

"During the war. They took it away afterwards." I faced him again. "Really, this has gone beyond a joke. You come here, ostensibly in search of information about the way in which Scheele spent his time in Bandaques, and when I've told you all I know you virtually charge me with his murder." I used my hands. "Where was I yesterday? Have I ever had a gun? ... It's fantastic. Utterly fantastic."

"Is it?" He rose, instinctively flicking ash from his tunic. "I would say that your refusal to answer a straightforward question more than excuses my having asked it."

Nonsensical though his suspicions were I supposed that it would be claimed that they were not without some justification. But the greater part of Monday and Tuesday was my preserve—Ilsa's too—and, because of her, I had no intention of sharing it with a third party.

I said: "I can only repeat that the last occasion I saw Scheele was on Monday night at the Bar Sinbad."

"What," he branched off, "did you think of him?"

"Did I like him, d'you mean?"

Romero nodded. "Exactly."

"No, I didn't."

With what he thought was cunning, he said: "Yet you were frequently in his company."

I countered: "There are many people I don't like, but they're still alive."

I was beginning to feel that there had never been a time when he wasn't either subjecting me to his scrutiny or moving about the room like a customer in a furniture store. He had started doing this again now and I said: "That ceramic isn't mine. I'm responsible for breakages here."

He put it down. "Why didn't you like him, señor?"

"For many reasons."

"And which of these reasons carried most weight with you?"

I said hotly: "You're banging your head against a wall. How many more times have I got to tell you that I had nothing— absolutely nothing—to do with Scheele's death?" It was coming up to seven o'clock, I noticed, and I fretted. "Why don't you leave me alone and do some of your groping elsewhere? You've allowed whoever did it enough start as it is."

"Where do you suggest I begin?"

"That's for you to decide. But I can assure you that you aren't being very clever at the moment." His silence provoked me into presenting an ultimatum. "Either show me better cause for wasting my evening—or go. I'll waive the apology."

Resentment sharpened his tone. "Very well, Señor Tyler. ... In the first place there is your interest—undenied by you—in Señora Scheele."

"That's not a crime."

"I carry a notebook; not a breviary." His smugness made me wince. "Secondly, there is your admitted dislike of the dead man. Thirdly, there is your reluctance to tell me how you spent the greater part of Monday, and your repeated refusal to account for your movements yesterday." He was working along his fingers. "Fourthly, I am taking into account a combination of minor facts—insignificant in themselves, perhaps, but of some consequence when considered in relation to everything else."

"Such as?"

He drew a long breath. "Your always being in Señora Scheele's company at critical times—last night, for instance; and again this morning. And your request to be present whenever she might be wanted in the future."

"Good God," I protested. "And you think that's suspicious? One day you'll suspect your own shadow."

He shrugged.

"Haven't you ever wanted to help someone? ... Besides, as you very well know, she doesn't speak Spanish."

His index finger was already touching the thumb of his opposite hand. I had grown tired of fencing with him. "Really," I said. "You'll have to do better than that. What other crass nonsense have you got lined up?"

"Fifthly, señor," he said, with the air of a man throwing an ace, "I have had it reported to me that, on Monday night, you and the dead man fought each other in the Bar Sinbad."

"It was hardly a fight."

"Everything is relative."

"He hit me and I hit him back—it was no more than that."

"What did you fight about?"

"He was drunk," I said.

"You hit him because he was drunk?"

"He hit me."

"Why?"

"We argued."

"What about?"

It was a minute after seven. "Look," I said, "I'm sick to death of this. You'll damn well have to wait for an answer."

I went to the telephone and got through to the España. "I want to speak to Señora Scheele," I said. "You'll find her in the American Bar." Half a minute later I was saying: "No? ... Well, will you please see she's told that Señor Tyler has just called and that he will be with her in a quarter of an hour?"

I snapped on some more lights, disturbed by not having made contact with her, wondering where she was.

Romero said: "You are a very impetuous man, señor."

"So?" My hands shook as I lit another cigarette. "Under your comic microscope I suppose, that always gets distorted into something significant?"

He let it pass. "You were on the point of explaining why you and the dead man had an argument."

"It wasn't about anything in particular. He was just in a filthy, carping mood. He usually was, anyhow."

"Why?"

"Maybe he was allergic to typewriters."

Romero frowned.

I explained. "His business was with typewriters—that's the reason he went to Barcelona. Perhaps he thought selling the things was beneath his dignity, perhaps the weather had got on his nerves, perhaps he was still brooding over being robbed—I don't know. I'm not a mind-reader. All I *do* know is that he was particularly unpleasant that night."

Romero smiled slightly with his mouth. "And because of typewriters and the weather and so on you are telling me he hit you?"

I shook my head. "It was because of something I said. I told him the past was a bucket of ashes."

"A bucket of ashes?" It was a disappointingly clumsy phrase in Spanish.

"Words to that effect. Old bones if you like. He kept talking about the war. He'd drunk too much and was growing tiresome and objectionable, so I tried to shut him up. My remark seemed to enrage him. That's all there was to it."

"I am expected to believe this?"

"I don't see why not. It happens to be the truth."

Romero switched a table-lamp on and off. He might have been on the point of saying: "I'll take this one. How much is it?" Instead, thoughtfully, he said: "Why didn't you mention this fight before?"

"Because it isn't of any consequence."

"No? ... What else haven't you told me, Señor Tyler?"

"Nothing that has any bearing on what happened to Scheele."

"You still refuse to discuss what you did with the rest of Monday, and on Tuesday?"

"That's right."

He suddenly gave me his undivided attention. "I am entitled to an answer and intend to get one."

"Not from me," I said.

"I have the authority to insist." He was entrenched in his quietest, most confident mood. "For instance, I have the authority—here and now—to ask you to surrender your passport."

"You can take it with pleasure. I'm only going as far as Bandaques."

"Then may I have it?"

He held out a hand. I wasn't sure whether he was bluffing, but I didn't much care. By that time I would have parted with almost anything to be rid of him.

"Of course," I said, and my willingness to relinquish it seemed to disarm him a little. "You're beginning to panic, capitán."

I opened the desk and took the passport from its pigeonhole. I also took out a pen and a sheet of paper and asked him for a receipt. I thought he might refuse, but he accepted the pen readily enough and wrote in a slanting scrawl: *Taken into custody this day one British passport No. 422196 property of Stephen Robert Tyler.* He added the date and, finally, with a spectacular flourish, signed his name: *Tomás Romero.*

Hoping in some way to discomfit him, I said: "Is there nothing else you want, or is the inquisition over?"

"Nothing now, señor."

"Your hat, perhaps?"

He still had another card to play and was therefore armoured against my tongue. "Before I go I would like to make your position quite clear. Let me just say that I have taken your passport more as a precaution than for any other reason—though it is also a pleasure for me to teach you a small lesson."

I suffered in silence.

"And a final thing—"

"Yes?"

"I shall be seeing Señora Scheele in the morning. You can break the news to her about her husband if you wish— I leave that to you. But do not imagine that tomorrow I will automatically accept her word when it confirms your own." He was very sure of himself now. "When I was younger and more vulnerable I might have done so, but nowadays, I assure you, I can smell collusion before it even comes through the door."

With difficulty I continued to be silent. I followed him into the hall; watched him ram on his preposterous hat.

Turning blandly on the step, he said: "And remember this, señor. To spare Señora Scheele embarrassment at a difficult time it will do you no good to telephone my office in a short while to state that on Tuesday you and she were in bed together. That may be the oldest alibi in the world—perhaps the most pleasant—but, unhappily, it is also one of the least impressive. Unless, that is, you happened to be in bed together in, say, the middle of the Plaza Mayor."

The starlight slowly dissolved him. I slammed the door and went back into the living-room. I suppose I had invited his parting shots, but that made them no easier to bear. As I poured myself another brandy I heard his car hiccoughing away over the gravel and my mind pursued him with a moment's abuse. All at once the quick bright glitter of my affair with Ilsa had been tarnished in a way that neither Scheele alive nor Scheele dead had succeeded in doing; ridiculed, somehow tainted. Romero's reasoning was crude and his methods amateurish, but there was a perspective to his thinking which contaminated.

The house was suddenly very quiet. I opened the windows on to the terrace in order to empty the room of tobacco-smoke and the sound of the laden sea beat in, slow and heavy. If it had not been for my anger I would probably have driven off to the España immediately Romero was clear. As it was I delayed for a couple of minutes. It was only ten past seven and I finished the brandy, then crossed to the telephone, wanting more than anything at that moment to talk with Ilsa so that I could arrive at the hotel freed from selfish anxieties as to her need of me. The indifference in her voice when we had last spoken lingered uneasily in my mind, and what I had to tell her now was shocking enough, brutally perplexing enough, to make her shrink even further into herself. I had come to accept that this was inevitable, but I still held to the hope that, given time, she could be drawn out again. Scheele would diminish—I hadn't ceased to believe that.

The smear of Romero's touch was already fading as I waited for the operator to put me through. The receptionist recognized me. "Señor Tyler?"

"Yes."

"I'm afraid we weren't able to get your message to Señora Scheele."

"Oh?" My heart sank a little. "Why was that?"

"She had gone to her room with the request that she did not wish to be disturbed. I wasn't aware of it when you called.

70

I had only just come on duty."

"I see." Seconds passed. Then: "Can you connect me with her now?"

"I am afraid not, señor. The request is still in force." Brightly she added: "Perhaps if you tried again in the morning?"

I put the handset back on the rest, hurt and humiliated. Ilsa's desire for isolation seemed aimed at me personally, and her manner of excluding me was even more wounding than her wish to do so. She could have called me, I thought bitterly. At least she could have let me know. ...

I walked through the room, nursing my dismay, and went out on to the terrace; stood under the vast white stars. A breath of air was moving furtively off the water and the faint smell of disaster came with it. I was trembling. In my imagination I heard Scheele's thick accents: "Real flesh and blood; real life and death. There's no substitute, Mister Tyler." And this time, aloud, I said to myself: "Why did you have to die at all? It was easier when you were alive."

2

When Ilsa arrived on the beach on Monday Scheele had already left for Barcelona. The previous night, as the fireworks which rounded off the procession split and streaked the sky, Scheele had grumbled: "How long's this likely to last? I'll need some sleep if I'm going to be any use in Barcelona tomorrow." Several times that day I had hovered on the brink of asking him whether the trip was still scheduled, but always I had hesitated for just too long and missed the suitable cues. His own silence about the visit—broken only when the fireworks were nearly at an end—had fed me with doubt and anxiety. Then, I had desperately wanted to hear it mentioned: have it confirmed. But on the Monday neither Ilsa nor I were once to refer to it—almost as if we believed we could thus deceive ourselves about his existence.

It was a brilliant morning. The sea was a flat calm and the sun had the sky to itself. Ilsa came at about ten, by which time I was already on the beach. When we saw one another we both started to run, and I remember that I laughed as I ran, splashing over the wet dark sand along the water's edge, filled with a crescendo of exhilaration that was like a burst of song. That she should be running too was somehow wonderful in itself, communicating her eagerness in a way that no words could have done.

When we were still a little apart she lost one of her sandals and stumbled; bent to retrieve it. She was hopping on one foot as I reached her, gaily trying to keep her balance while she struggled to get the sandal back on. Grasping her arm I was reminded of how slim she was, how fragile; but desire was muted with the sheer joy of again being with her. Breathless, she thanked me. "We've got a lovely day," she said, and her choice of phrase echoed everything I felt. The whole span of daylight was ours: while it lasted we were free, without restriction, alone.

"What d'you want to do?"

"I don't mind. You say." Her eyes shone.

"We could swim."

"I've no costume."

"Not underneath?" She was wearing tight, cream-coloured denim slacks and a short chequer-board shirt.

"I didn't think of it."

"A drive, then? We could take the car somewhere."

She nodded approval. "But not to anywhere in particular. Don't let's make any plans, Ty. Not today. Let it just happen."

Like a child I cupped my hands to the empty beach. "Any more for the mystery tour? Mystery tour starting in five minutes."

"What's a mystery tour?" she chuckled.

"They run them at home. Coach parties. Two-hour mystery tour, three bob. No one's supposed to know where he's going."

"Not even the driver?"

"He's blindfolded."

We linked hands, laughing, and walked up the slope towards the villa. It is impossible to measure happiness. But if one could draw a graph of it, record with certainty its endless rise and fall, that morning would stand out like a peak. I don't think that, for one moment, I consciously saw myself as a usurper. For too long I had accustomed myself to loneliness and was ill-fitted to cope with the sudden fire of the past few days: release from both was an intoxicant which destroyed the emptiness and jealousies of reality. For me, that morning, happiness was laughter and frivolous nonsense and the beauty of the day itself—all shared; and the knowledge that she had run to share them.

I drove north, away from Bandaques, and the wind streamed Ilsa's hair. Here and there, far out, the smooth cobalt sea was wrinkled a shade or two darker: a twist of smoke balanced on the taut line of the horizon. To our left the sierras were in their blurred, violet mood. Only when we came closer could we see through the deception—the harshness of the upper heights and the bare bones of exposed grey rock.

I sang:

> *Por de bajo del puento*
> *No pasa nadie,*
> *Tan solo el polvo*
> *Que lleva el aire ...*

Ilsa smiled. "Again." Instead, I spoke a translation:

> *Under the bridge*
> *Nobody goes,*
> *Only the dust*
> *That the wind blows...*

"I picked it up listening to Catalina—trills and all. Come on, you try it."

We took it line by line, half a dozen times, until she was tune and word perfect. I only knew one other verse and she mastered that as we corkscrewed through the pines away

73

from the metalled coast-road. We were climbing. The sea vanished and we began to feel the great strength of the enveloping hills; our own isolation. Once the trees ended we entered a diseased and inhospitable landscape of grass-tufted and precipitous slopes. We stopped singing, concentrating on pitted road and savage views.

Soon she said: "Somewhere nicer please, Mister Driver."

"Isn't this nice?"

"It's like the wrong side of the moon."

"I'm blindfolded, remember."

It was hard work at the wheel. The road twisted between the deformed breasts of hills, followed a ridge, then began a switchback descent into a valley. Scrawny goats littered the hillsides. A truck laden with timber ground up to meet us, lurched past, spewing dust and diesel fumes. Two men as ragged as scarecrows: an overburdened mule led by a boy. Otherwise our solitude continued. Miles away, along the narrow brown floor of the valley, villages nestled at the foot of blue, barren mountains like heaps of dumped stone. Nearer, smears of yellow broom merged into the tree-line. We plunged down through pines and chestnuts; found a surfaced road and were led between oleanders and tamarisks beside a swollen, khaki-coloured stream. Sugar cane grew here, and there were walled patches of reddish earth in which olive and almond trees stood in orderly rows. The first crumbling village came and went, then another spiked with poplars, its rotting edges somehow redeemed by clematis and splashes of crimson bougainvillea.

"Nice enough now?"

"Oh yes," Ilsa said. "It's beautiful. Sad and beautiful."

She sat very straight beside me, lips parted a little, occasionally turning her head when something or other particularly caught her eye. We said little, though even in the silences we seemed to be learning about each other. There would be a time for questions, for explanations, for exchanging an account of ourselves, but it had no place in the mood of that morning. We drove on, cruising slowly along the deep trench of the valley, singing again sometimes, laughing often, immersed in a happiness that seemed indestructible.

By noon we were nosing out of the valley, climbing once more. Somewhere near the crest a turn of the road exposed a small, tight village beside a spouting waterfall. But for the waterfall we might have passed through: instead we left the car and explored on foot. On a rocky platform below a squat, ochreous church we found a reed-covered shack where wine was sold. Benches and trestle tables were set outside and we sat there, watching the falling water fan out and whiten as it crashed on to black, glistening rock below. Some ragged children gathered to stare at us, fascinated, it seemed, by Ilsa's blonde hair. We drank a thin sherry from an unbranded bottle; chewed sweet, husky almonds. The bow-legged proprietor clattered in and out of the bead-curtains which covered the door, grinning, commenting on life and the weather, proudly producing his wife for our inspection. The place was too good to leave. The couple needed only the minimum of encouragement to provide us with a meal, and it was excellent—an omelette followed by red mullet, washed down with an amber-coloured wine. *"Bueno,"* we nodded time and again, to their obvious gratification. *"Bueno. Muy bueno."* The only thing to fail us was the sun. The first clouds pushed above the jagged skyline when we were half-way through the meal and by the time we were sipping our brandy they were thick and ugly. Continents of shadow began to blotch the hills.

"More rain, señor." The proprietor turned down the corners of his mouth. "There is no end to it. Soon we will need an Ark."

"We'll have to go," I said to Ilsa.

"I suppose so." She drained her glass reluctantly. "What a pity."

We paid and left. *"Adios,"* the man and his wife called after us. *"Sano y salvo."*

We waved back, turning in our tracks. "What's *sano y salvo?*" Ilsa asked.

"Safe and sound. ... *Adios. Gracias."*

Heavy drops hit us before we reached the car. The sun had vanished already and the air was going grey.

"It was wonderful there," Ilsa said. "So simple; so unexpected." She leaned her head against my shoulder as I went through the gears. "Is the driver still blindfolded?"

"Not any more."

"Mystery tour over?"

"Yes."

"Where are we going now?"

I kissed her lightly on the forehead and desire pushed through me. "Home," I said.

We were quieter on the return run. The rain had so reduced visibility that driving demanded all my attention. I was glad when we found a metalled surface; gladder still when I eventually discovered our whereabouts. Once, peering past the wipers as I slowed at a junction, an arrowed sign thrust itself at me: BARCELONA—and I remember with what swift success my mind disposed of the intrusion. Bandaques was then only a dozen or so miles away and they didn't take us long. By a quarter to three we were through the town and heading along the dunes to the Villa Miramar.

"Even in the rain it looks lovely," Ilsa said.

I smiled. "You're easy to please today."

"I'm happy, Ty—that's why. Very, very happy."

At the house we ducked from car to porch. I followed Ilsa inside and turned on the living-room radio: a local station was pumping out soft, innocuous music.

"Catalina's deserted us. Drinks are on the table if you'd like one. I won't be a minute: I'm going to put the car away."

When I came back she was standing under the awning on the terrace, turning the pages of my manuscript.

"Did you write this?"

"What?"

"This." She pointed, and I read: *We are swords that spirits fight with. We never see the hands that brandish us.*

"No," I said. "That's too good to be mine; I just jotted it down. But it's a sort of theme to what I'm doing."

76

"It's not true, Ty."

"What isn't?"

"What it says."

"No?"

"No," she said.

Her sidelong gaze was strangely disturbing. For a fleeting duration I was aware only of its gravity; puzzled by the change in her. Then I realized that she was nervous; consumed with a burning uncertainty. It had destroyed the softness of her eyes and quivered on her lips. The sound of the rain and the music seemed to swell: desire moved urgently in me again like something that had lain in wait for too long. I heard myself say: "Does it matter? Let's argue about it some other—" and suddenly I was lost in the sensation of her mouth and body against mine. She had come to me as much as I to her and this time there was no gentle pushing away; no forced curbing of passion. Her hands, her lips, her tongue were as eager as mine. Under the drumming awning and in the bedroom we gave up our secrets, and both times, when it was too quickly over, she was generous with understanding. In between, and afterwards, spinning her soft hair in my hands, our limbs slack, brushing our kisses gently, her small, boyish face bore an expression of shyness which somehow convinced me that this had never happened to her before; that I was the first stranger.

"Why me?" I asked her. "Why me, Ilsa?"

She closed her eyes, burrowed her face into my shoulder, but she didn't answer, and the moment of wonder passed away. I was too content, too drugged, to attempt to retain it.

Later, propped on one elbow, marvelling once more at the smoothness of her slender brown and white body, knowing that I would want her again as soon as she had gone, I said: "Try and see me tomorrow."

"Perhaps," she said.

"Please." I kissed the small blue vein in her neck. "You must."

"If I can," she said.

It was the nearest we came to admitting openly that what had gone before was stolen, like the day itself. Even when time forced us to dress it was Catalina's name which intruded, not Scheele's. She was due at five o'clock and we left the house a few minutes before the hour. Everything glistened but it had stopped raining; when, I had no idea. I drove Ilsa back to the hotel, slowly, dragging out what little was left of our solitude. And there we parted, at the foot of the steps, under the watchful eye of the doorman. There was no sign of the cream Mercedes but the pavements were busy with people, the street noisy with the blare of horns, the belch of exhausts. It was no place to linger. Only in our minds could we still cling to each other.

"Good-bye, Ilsa."

A look, a nod. "Dear Ty." Then she was gone and the doorman was telling me it was safe to pull out.

"*Buenas tardes, señor. ... Gracias.*"

The last person I wanted—or expected—to see that evening was Scheele. But, more than ever, the house seemed a desolate place, and after bearing with it for as long as I could I went into Bandaques. It was nearer ten than nine when I got there. I had nothing in mind—only a need to destroy loneliness. The restaurants and pavement cafés were packed and the cinema by the amphitheatre was sucking in its last-house audience. I took a brandy at one of the seedy cafés near the bullring and watched with envy the couples who sauntered past or sat nearby. Even if they weren't going to bed together they could at least parade themselves in public. I let a shoe-black kneel at my feet and produce a shine that would have rivalled Romero's; refused offers of American cigarettes and a bargain-price watch. A blind lottery-ticket seller moaned his way through the tables and because his milk-white stare moved me to pity I bought from him. He said automatically: "You will be lucky, señor. This time you will be lucky." And I thought: Will I? Will I? What do you know about luck?

78

I left and went elsewhere; walked the streets, stared into shop windows, was cannoned into by people with destinations. Joaquin greeted me at the Bar Sinbad, fussed over me, eager to practise his English. He had an El Greco face; long, grey, fine-boned.

"You know Browning, señor? Robert Browning?"

"Some, yes."

"A gentleman was drinking here now from England. Ten minutes ago. He says Robert Browning is very beautiful."

"I wouldn't recommend him, Joaquin."

"No?"

"Not for you."

"He is not beautiful?"

"Difficult."

"And Lord Byron? This gentleman also tells me—"

"Try Wordsworth," I said.

He was signalled to another table: departed shaking his head. Two women came in; hesitated by the empty chairs. One said to me: "With your permission?" and I nodded. "It's all yours. I'm about to go."

I sank my brandy and stood up; started towards the exit. Then a thick voice separated itself from all the others and I heard my name called.

It was Scheele. I stopped in my tracks, knowing how the guilty feel when challenged.

"Mister Tyler!"

He was slightly drunk; I could tell as much before I discovered where he was sitting. For half a moment I thought with relief that he was alone: then I saw that Ilsa was with him. I waved a perfunctory greeting, hoping to escape, to be spared facing them together, but he lurched to his feet and pushed heavily past a waiter.

"Come and join us, Mister Tyler."

"Thanks, but I was just leaving."

I started on some rigmarole about an appointment, but he brushed it aside. His huge grip closed on my arm.

"You're always refusing me. I'll begin to think you don't

like me or something." He swayed; laughed. "Ten minutes won't matter whoever she is."

Short of wrenching myself away I had no choice. People stared as he led me in Ilsa's direction. I could hardly bear to look at her and her tense, desperately improvised smile somehow increased the agony.

She managed to say: "Good evening, Ty."

"Your husband seems to have arrested me."

"He was running away somewhere," Scheele boomed, slurring the words. He called for another chair. "What do you drink?"

"Fundador." Then, lamely: "But I really mustn't stay."

"Nonsense." He ordered imperiously. I was wary as I sat down, unable to fathom his mood, loathing every second.

"I've been to Barcelona, Mister Tyler."

"Oh yes?"

"You told Ty last night you were going," Ilsa put in and I wondered if it were wise. I caught her gaze. She frowned and shook her head, both minutely, as much as to say: "It's all right."

"You've been there, I suppose?" Scheele steam-rollered on.

"Several times."

"It's a lousy, stinking place."

I shrugged, not prepared to be drawn: I was used to his adjectives.

"A lousy, stinking place full of lousy, stinking people."

"It sounds as if you've had a bad day."

"A bad day is correct." He advanced his elbows towards me; brought his face closer. The pale, thick-lidded eyes were blood-shot. "I've been dealing with little men. Little men without memories. You don't know what it's like, Mister Tyler. You work alone. You don't have to humiliate yourself."

Ilsa said: "Erich."

"Some people don't mind humiliating themselves. You've seen them: so have I." He rinsed whisky round his mouth; swallowed. "I am not that kind—least of all here."

"Erich," she repeated.

A guitar twanged in the background: a hoarse, sad voice, like the cry from a minaret, lifted above the hubbub:

> *Cada vez considero*
> *Que me tengo que more ...*

Scheele ignored her; leaned near enough for me to see the small hairs which sprouted on his nose. "Memories are important, Mister Tyler. They last longer than friends." The words came slip-shod; tongue-heavy. "Don't you agree?"

For want of something better, I said: "You can't live in the past."

He laughed silently; lifted his glass. Whisky spilled from it, staining the cloth. A waiter came and mopped up. Scheele focused on him blearily. *"Sprechen Sie deutsch?"*

"No, señor. No deutsch."

I made an attempt to leave, but Scheele restrained me. "Fundador," he said to the waiter. "Another Fundador for the Englishman."

Ilsa said: "You mustn't force Ty to stay if he doesn't want to."

We exchanged glances uneasily, like prisoners in the same dock. But Scheele's hand still rested on my arm and I wanted to extricate myself quietly; without a scene. I was contemptuous of him but I wasn't gloating. In this mood he provoked an aversion that somehow destroyed any feelings of triumph or pity—even of jealousy. But it was bad to be there all the same, a cheating thing, and I despised myself.

He continued: "Were you ever a soldier, Mister Tyler?"

"Of necessity."

"You know something about it then."

"About what?"

"Obedience. Discipline. Authority." He made a mess of each word.

"In a small way."

"Authority. ... Respect," he added.

"I didn't exactly run the war."

Inadvertently my fingers touched Ilsa's as I knocked ash from my cigarette and I knew I couldn't stand the pretence much longer.

"But you were a soldier?"

"Yes."

"I was also a soldier, Mister Tyler. We have common ground, eh?—something we share."

Ilsa rose abruptly, gathered up her bag, and excused herself. Her face was very pale in the smoky light as she turned away. I thought: God, why did I ever come in here?

Scheele dragged at my sleeve with the insistence of a dog. "Something in common," he slurred.

"It was a long while ago."

"But you can remember it. It's not forgotten."

"Some things are never forgotten." I was free to match him now; release my animosity. "A week after I was married my wife was killed by one of your bombs."

His glazed eyes narrowed. "That's bad," he said. "Bad." He paused for a moment, but the obsession festering in his mind swiftly repossessed him, obliterating any drunken trace of sympathy. He was looking through me, as if I weren't there. "Respect," he said. "Respect is important. ... We had it once."

"We?" I hated him.

He didn't seem to hear. *"Todo o nada.* ... All or nothing. Is that right, Mister Tyler? All or nothing?"

"I don't understand you."

"Nada. Nada. Nada." He thumped the table. "For them it was *nada.* Nothing."

I said quickly: "I must go."

"Stay and talk," he pleaded. There was applause as the singer finished his song.

"Some other time."

"We were only just getting started." He tried to summon a waiter but I restrained him. "We've a lot in common."

"You flatter yourself."

It went home; pierced his stupor. He pushed back his chair and hauled himself to his feet.

I went on: "The past's a bucket of ashes. A pile of rubble. Incinerator dust. You ought to know. You made it, you and the rest of your—"

I wasn't expecting the blow. It caught me on the left side of the head, just above the ear. I was more surprised than hurt. I staggered, then countered instinctively, hitting him solidly in the chest. Somewhere close a girl cried out. Scheele grunted and slumped back into his chair, almost tilting it over. His mouth fell open and he blinked up at me in dazed amazement. I saw Joaquin and another white-coated waiter converging on us but I was moving before they reached our table. I walked past Scheele, shouldered between a couple of men who'd jack-in-the-boxed to their feet, and stormed out into the street.

For a while I walked anywhere; anywhere to get clear. My head buzzed, seemed ballooned to twice its size, and I muttered to myself as I pushed through the thinning crowds. I had a vague, short-lived feeling of satisfaction. But, soon, my anger turned against myself and I fretted lest I had ruined the chance of another meeting with Ilsa. The thought nagged at me on the way home, kept me awake until the small hours, disturbed what sleep I could find—more, even, than the pain of knowing that she was with him in the Hotel España.

But next day she came and I apologized, relief making me repetitive. We finished:

"It should never have happened. My tongue gets the better of me at times."

"I thought you were very patient."

"I never expected you'd be in the Bar Sinbad, but it was stupid of me to go there anyhow. Stupid and thoughtless."

"Don't let's talk about it any more."

"All right. But I'm desperately sorry."

Whatever self-deception we had managed to achieve on the Monday was no longer possible. Now we openly acknowledged Scheele; met despite him. "Where's he gone?" I asked, and Ilsa said: "Somewhere called Gondra."

In anticipation of her coming I had given Catalina the day off, but it was almost noon before the clouds which massed overnight had discharged their load and moved away; a quarter of an hour later before my anxiety ended and I saw Ilsa on the beach. She was very quiet to begin with, needing time, it seemed to adjust herself to a more blatant conspiracy. But her gaiety gradually broke through and we found laughter again: if hers was a trifle strained, a little less frequent, I wasn't aware of it. We prepared a cold lunch together, danced on the terrace to the radio, lay naked on the bed—and for me the only difference in the two days was that Scheele was inescapable. Even when I made love to her it was as if I believed I was hurting him. Triumph, jealousy—I knew them then. Even when I told her: "I love you, Ilsa. I love you," his shadow fell across us, for I remembered with dismay that in a matter of days they would be going home.

Late in the afternoon, limp from it all, I was to say: "Don't go with him, Ilsa. Stay here with me."

She traced the line of my lips with a finger.

"Will you?"

She was silent for a long while, studying my face with grave intensity. "You mustn't push me, Ty," she said at last, and at the time it seemed answer enough.

We left the house at about six and drove to the hotel. I wouldn't have stayed but for the crowd in the lobby and the news of the Lareo Dam. Looking back it is easy to be mistaken about what one really felt at some particular juncture. Every hour that passes adds to its distortion. But I honestly believe that, as we waited, I knew subconsciously that I would never see Scheele alive again.

3

Lights glittered along the promontory; winked meaningless signals. I heard a bat squeak on the wing; watched a star plunge to its death. Time had passed since dismay propelled me on to the terrace. The bitter hurt had lost its bite; the smart had gone and I was beginning to think about tomorrow.

Tomorrow morning I would tell Ilsa about Scheele, choosing my words, anticipating her distress. Romero could imagine what he liked; she at least would know how wide of the mark he was. Perhaps I could build on that. Tomorrow I would say: "Ilsa, I don't know how to tell you this, but I'd rather you heard it from me than from Romero. ..." And before long, inevitably, disbelief would frame the self-same questions which had earlier sprung from me:

"Who would want to shoot him?" And: "Why?"

CHAPTER FIVE

I WENT early to the España. A few dead goats, washed up overnight, littered the beach; inshore, the sea bed had the consistency of a red-brown stew. Several men were scrounging about near the water's edge, though God knows what they hoped to find.

Ilsa was in the section of the dining-room set aside, at that hour, for breakfast. Because it was early I had somehow expected having to wait for her to come down from her room and was unprepared to find myself immediately directed to her table. That Scheele had been murdered had become, for me, an accepted fact, and all at once it seemed fantastic that she was still in ignorance of it. As I crossed to her corner I felt unsure of myself; in need of more time to rehearse what she must be told.

She looked up. "I wondered if you would come."

"May I join you?"

"Of course." She offered the sad trace of a smile, but whatever hope flickered in me was offset by the deadness of her tone.

She said: "I'm sorry about last night. I just felt I had to go to bed. All the people in the bar, talking, laughing—I couldn't bear it. ... Did they tell you?"

"When I rang they did." The sense of pique hadn't quite gone. "I could have been here by seven-fifteen."

"There wouldn't have been any point, Ty"—which, with a momentary renewal of bitterness, I took to mean: "I didn't want you anyway."

A waiter arrived and I ordered coffee. A man with a crabred face at the next table read something aloud from the *Daily Express* while the woman with him stared morosely at her finger-nails.

"Romero delayed me."

"Romero?"

"He called at the house and kept me for well over an hour. Otherwise—"

"I've had a message from him."

She let me see it. To my surprise it was in English, and I could only imagine that he'd put it together with the aid of a dictionary: typed it himself, too, probably. I read:

Please to present yourself at my office by 10.30 hours of this Thursday morning for particular questions in concern of your husband great tragedy.

His flamboyant signature had driven the pen-nib through the flimsy green paper.

"Will you go with me?"

"You know I will." I was balanced between hope and dread, desperately anxious to win back a little ground before she was lost to me again in the welter of shocked confusion that was coming to her. "I'll do anything—always. I've told you a dozen times."

She nodded her thanks, but abstractedly, as if I'd done no more than light her cigarette. The professional observer in me heard the man at the next table chuckle and say: "Osbert Lancaster's damned good today"; caught the woman's flat: "Oh, yes?"

"What do you imagine Romero wants me for?" Ilsa's eyes were without lustre, as if she had undergone a fever.

I hesitated.

"What did he come to see you about last night?"

"Erich," I said. It was strange to find myself using Scheele's first name: I had never done it before. The woman complained as she returned the *Express* to her companion: "I don't think it's funny at all." I pushed my cup aside. "Ilsa, there's something you've got to know. ..." And suddenly I was telling her, badly, the thought-out way of doing it forgotten in the face of her incredulous stare and barely audible interjections.

I reached out and placed a hand on hers; identified myself with her bewilderment. When it came to it I was surprised by how little I knew. Shot not drowned, dead before the dam broke; no water in lungs, wallet intact. ... That was about all: a few sentences covered everything. But half an hour later I was still trying to guide Ilsa towards belief in what had happened. The man and woman near us left; other tables filled and emptied. Our coffee remained un-tasted and grew cold. And Ilsa kept saying things like: "It doesn't make sense. ... We'd only been here a few days and hardly knew anyone. ... I don't understand: I just don't understand. ... It must have been an accident—some sort of accident. There's no other explanation. ..."

The previous day seemed to have drained her of emotion. Only once did tears briefly fill her eyes. I watched her earnestly, selfishly. The door between us remained shut fast, as I had feared it would. For all her bewilderment she was remarkably self-possessed. I felt that her defencelessness was going—not because I was present, but because she was involved in another world where she didn't really need me at all. I was the Boy Scout again—someone who could translate when she met Romero; run errands, offer advice, a wall against which she could throw her questions in the hope of a worthwhile answer bouncing back. Vanity urged me to argue: "He's dead, Ilsa. Whether he was shot or drowned doesn't matter. He only died once: you must only grieve once." But I was afraid, lest a chance phrase should violate her memory of him. Instead, seeking in some other way to earn myself merit, I said: "Romero thinks I did it."

Her forehead puckered as she quoted me: "'Did it'? ... What do you mean?"

"He thinks I had something to do with Erich's death."

"You can't be serious."

"*He* is. He's gone so far as to impound my passport."

"Im-pound?"

"Taken possession of it."

"But why?"

88

"He's got his reasons. What happened in the Bar Sinbad on Monday night is one. Mainly, though, it's because I refused to tell him where I was on Tuesday."

"Why should he even ask?" she began, but the sentence never went beyond half way. Her tired eyes widened a fraction. In the long pause that followed I watched the shape of Romero's logic slowly dawn in her mind; her cheeks colour.

"Oh, Ty," she said at length. "I'm sorry"—and I remember how appalled, how laden with personal guilt she made it sound, as if it were the cause more than the effect that she regretted.

"Romero's a fool," I said. "He'll come to his senses in time. Meanwhile he's like a dog worrying the only bone in sight. Don't concern yourself on my account." I laid my hand on hers again, but there was no response. "And don't tell him anything you don't want to. What he expects from me is an alibi, independent witnesses—the usual thing. That's the irony of it."

"What are you going to do?"

I shrugged, "At least *you* know it wasn't me."

"I will tell him so."

"He won't believe you, Ilsa. Not in his present mood."

We were quiet for a while and I could tell that her attentions were elsewhere—wandering in the maze where my news had brought her. I had trodden the same paths throughout the night and could almost trace the circling course of her thoughts.

"What time is it?" she asked suddenly.

"Ten-ten. The car's outside: there's no hurry."

But she was restless and wanted to go. In the car, she said: "Is that all Romero is doing?—just checking on you?"

"Last night it was. He's obsessed by the fact that I had a motive."

Without warning her self-control left her: her hands went to her face and she cried. "Oh God," she sobbed. "What's happened? What's happened suddenly?"

I wanted to bite off my tongue. "Ilsa," I said. "Ilsa."

I doubt if she heard me or felt my touch, but every shudder of her shoulders seemed to carry along my arm and reverberate in my heart. By the time we reached Romero's office she had recovered, but her eyes were raw. We had six or seven minutes to spare and we waited in silence while she fiddled nervously with mirror and handkerchief. Silence was best: I had run out of words.

Eventually, when she'd put her dark glasses back on, I said: "Ready now?" and she nodded.

The smell of must greeted us. In the sunless light by the barrier I spoke to the duty-sergeant. He nodded curtly; opened the pass-gate. I was about to follow Ilsa through but he raised his hand.

"Not you, señor."

"Why not?"

"I have been instructed."

"The lady doesn't speak Spanish," I protested. "Someone needs to be with her."

"Captain Romero has made the necessary arrangements."

"I should like to see him, please."

"He is unobtainable at present."

"Not here, d'you mean?"

"Here, but unobtainable."

I could have struck him for the relish with which he delivered it. "It's no good, Ilsa. Romero wants you on your own. He's got someone with him who'll translate." I pressed against the barrier. "I'll wait for you. I'll wait in the Bar Sinbad."

"All right."

The sergeant said: "Come with me, please," and started along the cooridor.

"Ilsa."

She glanced back wearily, yet with a willingness that implied a continuing need of me. "Yes?"

"Try not to be hurt by anything Romero says. We'll get to the truth one day, even if we have to do it ourselves."

For a moment I thought she was going to speak. But in the end all she did was nod, gravely, as if filled with a sudden resolve. I watched her follow the sergeant to Romero's door and go in. Then I turned from the barrier and walked, blinking, into the sunlight, feeling like a deserter.

The Bar Sinbad was diagonally across the square: I drove round and parked the car under a dusty plane tree. Joaquin greeted me almost as soon as I'd sat at one of the outside tables.

"Good morning, Mister Tyler. How are you today?" I wasn't in the mood to give an English lesson and didn't answer. He said: "The book goes bad?"

"It's not the book."

"No?"

I could just see the entrance to the Civil Guard headquarters between the trees. "Bring me a coffee, will you, Joaquin?"

"With milk?"

"Black."

He found a reason to dust the cloth with his napkin. "I have read Wordsworth." (He pronounced it "reed".)

"Good for you."

He must have thought I doubted him, for he declaimed:

> "A primrose by a river's brim
> A yellow primrose was to him,
> And it was nothing more—

That is beautiful, Mister Tyler. Very much beautiful."

"I'm glad you like it." I thought: Romero can't keep her long. Half an hour at most, surely. ...

"What is a primrose?"

"A flower."

"In Spanish."

"Primrose? ... I'm sorry, Joaquin, but I don't honestly know."

"Even so it is beautiful," Joaquin insisted loyally.

"Yes." She ought to be out by eleven, I thought.

"Coffee with milk?"

"Without," I said. *"Negro."*

91

He went away. Pigeons pecked in the gutters. A coachload of tourists went by, heading for The White Caves. A nun left the street and came to my table, collecting for the poor. She was young, her face unlined, her smile of thanks innocently generous, and I envied her with sudden intensity because she would never know another person's body; would never be shared.

"Black coffee, Mister Tyler—and a Fundador."

"I only asked for coffee."

"The Fundador is with the compliments of Joaquin. You look like coffee is not enough."

It pleased him that I should take it. *"Salud."*

He said: "The señora is with Captain Romero?"

"How d'you know that?" I was more sharp than I realized.

He bent his knees a little until his head was level with mine; nodded through the planes. "I see you both come in the car. Both go in. Only you come out." He spread his hands disarmingly. "There is no magic, Mister Tyler. Only what I see."

I looked at my watch and was dismayed to find that it wasn't even ten-forty.

"It was bad about Señor Scheele," Joaquin said. The tables he served were empty: there was no one to take him away. "Very, very tragical."

I couldn't be bothered to correct him. I had forgotten that I hadn't been to the Bar Sinbad since the Monday night and was vaguely discomfited to realize that the last Joaquin had seen of me was elbowing my way out of the place after punching Scheele in the chest.

"There is much talk now about the Lareo Dam." He depressed the corners of his lips. "A scandal, maybe."

"So I've heard."

Waiters have a natural capacity for concealment. I often wondered, when we talked together, how much knowledge Joaquin held back. As always, his long El Greco face was no guide.

"It is a terrible thing for the señora. For him to be there

on that day!" He clucked his tongue. "On that very day. Ayee —that is bad."

"Mister Scheele was a great sight-seer." The dark doorway across the square remained empty. I remembered Ilsa's words: "Every brick, every stone. ..."

"What is there to see at Gondra? It was a forgotten place before the waters came—not even on the maps." Joaquin raised his hands chest-high; started moving them forward towards a point of collision. "How is it called in English, Mister Tyler, when this happens?" My frown made him continue: he moved his hands once more. "I do not mean accident. I mean English for: What makes accident?"

"Chance. ... Fate."

He selected "Chance"; sampled it out loud.

Chance was an animal which killed when it was hungry; I remembered the phrase from somewhere.

"Kismet, if you like." I thought: The Moor in you should know that.

I glanced through the plane trees; looked at my watch. Ten forty-six. Time was playing its malicious tricks again.

Joaquin cleared his throat, came nearer. "The señora," he began. "You think she would like the ring back?"

"What ring?"

"Señor Scheele's ring."

I stiffened slightly. For the first time in days I felt a tremor of excitement. But I didn't look up.

"It was stolen," I said guardedly.

"I believe."

"There were other things stolen, too. A watch and a lighter."

He queried. "Lighter?"

"Un mechero. Talk in Spanish," I said.

"I know only of the ring."

"What became of the other things?"

"I think they were sold."

"To whom?"

"That I don't know." He flipped at a fly. "It is regretted."

"Who sold them?"

"A friend of mine."

"And this same friend has the ring?"

"I am told."

Just when I least wanted it to happen he was summoned to a nearby table. I waited impatiently, trying to recall what Scheele had told me on the night of the theft. He'd suspected the hotel staff, and I wondered whether Joaquin's friend was another waiter. A car drew up outside the Civil Guard building and a man got out; disappeared through the door. The guard on duty rested his rifle between his legs and leaned against the wall: his hat was designed for the purpose.

Ilsa had been there twenty minutes now. ...

Joaquin returned; bribed me with another brandy. "You think the señora will be interested?"

"I expect it will depend on the price."

"There is no price."

"Either your friend's a sentimentalist or he doesn't know gold when he sees it."

"I can't answer for him. But I know he will return it if it would please the señora."

"You're taking a big risk," I said. "Captain Romero would be very interested. I could report you."

"You'd never do that, señor." His features crinkled sympathetically. "Besides, you are in sufficient trouble as it is."

I raised an eyebrow; paused. "This mysterious friend of yours, Joaquin. You can trust me."

"I've never doubted it."

"Do I know him?"

"From about three months ago."

It was easier to ask than to rack my brains. "Who is he, then?"

Joaquin lowered his voice. "Luis Zavella, señor. You remember him?"

Yesterday, to Romero, I had denied knowledge of Zavella, but only to save time. There had been no ulterior motive.

Yes, I remembered him: we had met at the Villa Miramar, though it wasn't an orthodox encounter. The novel had entered one of its periodic bad patches. Late one evening, after a particularly abortive day, I walked the beach for an hour or more, hoping that—as so oftens happens—the difficulties would somehow resolve themselves if I gave them their head. It was a warm, cloudless night with a waxing moon which cast shadows as strong and clear-cut as many a spring day's in England. Bandaques pulsed brightly: to the left of the promontory, far out, a liner moved—as compact and remote as the Pleiades.

Around nine, I started back towards the house. No lights were on and its moon-washed walls gave it an unreal, two-dimensional quality. I approached through the beach-gate, crossed the garden and mounted the steps to the terrace. There was no sound except for the rhythmic wash of the sea: everything was rigidly still, duplicated in patterns of blue shade. But when I was only a few yards from the door an unidentified noise made me pause. I waited, head cocked, wondering if it would be repeated. Seconds later it was and I realized that someone had coughed inside the house. It was a man's cough, dry and rasping, and as far as I could judge it came from the living-room.

I was wearing sandals and had therefore moved quietly, but I was quieter still as I edged to the wall beside the door. There was a tightness in my chest and the moonlight seemed to bounce with the thump of my heart. I dared not attempt to peer inside lest whoever was there saw my silhouette: in any case the awning was down and the room was in shadow. Just out of reach, close to the typewriter, was a cigarette-lighter designed in imitation of a seventeenth-century flint-lock pistol. Alarmed though I was I couldn't repress a sense of the melodramatic as I crouched down and made a long arm for it. Upright again, flat against the wall, I tensed myself for the only practical course open to me. For a long moment I delayed, rehearsing in my mind exactly what I was going to do: then, sucking in a deep breath, I yanked the door open and flicked on every light in the room.

The man bending over my desk reacted as if he had received an electric shock. He swung round violently, hands jerking wide, and a half-shout, half-grunt came from him. With a prickle of relief I saw that he was unarmed. He remained absolutely motionless, a scarecrow figure, pressed back against the desk as though he'd been impaled.

"What are you doing here?"

My voice shook. I had little confidence in the thing in my hand. I saw his eyes fasten on to it, move rapidly in search of ways of escape, then return to the level of my right hip.

"Who are you? What d'you want?"

Life seemed to re-enter his limbs. His arms fell slackly to his sides and he straightened up, his whole bearing one of sudden resignation.

"Who are you?" I repeated.

"Someone who shouldn't be here."

It was a disconcerting reply, all the more so because it was accompanied by a rueful smile. He was younger than I'd at first thought—about thirty; handsome in a lean, haggard sort of way. Unshaven, hollowed cheeks made him seem older—that, and a hunted look which even the smile didn't succeed in eradicating.

I told him to stand over against the wall and was almost surprised when he obeyed. He moved on the balls of his feet, as easily as a cat.

"What's your name?"

"Does it matter?"

It didn't in the least, but I saw no sense in agreeing with him. "I want to know."

"Luis Zavella."

"Turn your pockets out on the floor."

"It would be a waste of time." He spoke with a natural bravado which was somehow inoffensive.

"Turn them out," I said.

He did so. He wore no jacket; only a blue shirt and corduroy trousers. They yielded little—a few single peseta notes, three chestnuts, a rag of cloth, a small knife with a broken blade, matches, some loose cigarettes. There was nothing belonging to me or to the house. He coughed twice before he was through, a bone-dry cough that arched his back.

"Is that all?"

"I am afraid so." He smiled again, with a sad frankness. "You returned too early, señor. Otherwise I would have made a better showing."

"I've no doubt."

With a shrug of defeat, he said: "I would rather you kept the pesetas than let Captain Romero have them. The cigarettes, too."

"He knows you of old, I suppose."

"By sight only. Not to shake hands with exactly."

He seemed harmless enough; even likeable. I was beginning to feel a little foolish pointing the cigarette-lighter at him. He coughed again. It was an ugly sound and I told him to go to the alcove and pour himself a brandy. He gazed at me doubtfully, eyes watering from the spasm.

"Go on," I said. "There's no trick." Then, impulsively: "This thing isn't a gun, anyhow."

I laid it on the table. He rubbed his slightly hooked nose in astonishment: laughed uneasily. "You are tempting me, señor."

"I shouldn't try anything if I were you."

"On the contrary—if you were me you would."

"Have the brandy first." Mystified, he hesitated. "Go on," I repeated. "And get one for me while you're about it. Don't worry—I've no intention of phoning the Civil Guard."

Relief eased his features in a way that was disturbing to watch. "What, then?" He was suspicious even of mercy.

"I'd like to talk."

"I am not much of a talker."

"A few questions, that's all."

"What about?"

"You."

"Then I can go?" He was still slightly incredulous.

"Yes."

As if it explained everything, he said: "I am Luis Zavella."

"So you told me. Where d'you live?"

"Here—there." He moved his hands to great effect. "Many places."

"What d'you do?"

"It depends."

"On what?"

"On how hungry I am."

"Are you married?"

"No." The cough shook him again, but he smiled when it left him. "I am nothing, señor. Just a thief. Not worth your while."

"Were you never anything else?"

"A boy. Long ago."

He turned from me, as if hurt by a memory, and went to the alcove; poured the brandies. Close-to, when he handed me mine, I could see that he was ill. There was a sickly pallor beneath the gipsy skin.

"*Salud,*" he said, dark eyes holding my gaze. "And my thanks. You are a strange man."

"Strange?"

"Captain Romero would never forgive you if he could see us now."

"I'll probably never even meet the gentleman."

"Then you are lucky."

Clinically, I said: "Will you, d'you think?"

"One day. If it isn't him it will be someone else. Time is an ambush, señor. It wins in the end."

He couldn't relax for long. I tried to keep him talking, wondering what I would learn. Everything is grist to the mill. But he was as tense as an animal in a pen, even though he knew the locks were off. It seemed a cruelty to keep him. After about ten minutes I gave him some food from the refrigerator and showed him to the door.

By way of insurance, I said: "I'm not a fool, Zavella. And I'm not sorry for you. Don't mistake what's happened tonight

98

for kindness. If you ever want to come here again, ring the bell. Understand?"

"Yes, señor." His face was quite green under the moon as he held out a hand. *"Hasta la vista."*

A moment later he was a shadow amongst shadows, only the diminishing sound of his cough marking his route. And I wandered back inside to write a piece about him in my notebook before his image and choice of words lost their clarity.

"Yes," I said to Joaquin. "I remember Zavella."

"He remembers you. He asked me to speak with you— seeing that you know the señora so well."

I could swallow the insinuation. I had needed to deceive only Scheele, and Scheele was dead. Heads turned when Ilsa and I were together—I noticed them now; but while he lived I had been blinkered by my own intent.

I knocked a cigarette from the packet: Joaquin was the quicker with the match. "It stands to reason she'll want the ring back."

"Then I shall tell Luis."

"And I'll get it from you, is that it?"

"I expect."

"When?" I asked.

"It is impossible to say. Perhaps tomorrow. Perhaps in three or four days."

"When did he first make this offer?"

"Yesterday."

"Not before?"

"No."

"He was in town on Saturday night," I said.

"I know. But he never came to me." Joaquin seemed to feel that some explanation was necessary. "Luis is a cousin of mine. I try to help him when I can. He has had a poor life." He paused reflectively; changed his tack. "I should not like you to think that I approve of what he does, señor. In particular I should not like you to think that I enjoy speaking to you in this fashion about Señor Scheele's ring. Yet Luis isn't a bad person at heart."

The plane trees were shedding tiny showers of yellow pollen. A man prodded some indignant turkeys along the pavement with a stick: children splashed in the marble basin of the central fountain. It was eleven o'clock and there was still no sign of Ilsa.

A newcomer snapped his fingers and Joaquin reacted as if jerked by a string. For a brief spell I gave my mind to Zavella, casting back to our meeting, then to the chase after him through the procession and watching crowds. Strangely, I had never thought of him in connection with the robbery: nor when Romero had mentioned his name did I link it with the memory of Scheele's heavy facetiousness at the time of the disturbance. I found it odd and somewhat ironic that he, of all people, should be the culprit. But what fascinated was his wish to return the ring. Why? Because of his reprieve that night at the Villa Miramar? And why only the ring? Had he sold the other things before word reached him of Scheele's death? Was he, in fact, a sentimentalist, regretful suddenly, anxious to make a gesture of amends?

"Joaquin."

"Yes, Mister Tyler." He was free again.

"Stick to Spanish," I said. "I want to get this absolutely straight."

"Sí, señor."

"What did you mean a short while ago when you said that I was in trouble?"

He hesitated sufficiently to give the slight pause significance. "I hear things."

"From over there?" I nodded towards the Civil Guard building.

"Sometimes."

"Captain Romero?"

"Now you are joking, señor."

"Did you hear what sort of trouble I was supposed to be in?"

100

"Only that you have been interrogated."

"D'you know why?"

He hedged: "For what reason, do you mean?"

"Yes. I mean precisely that."

It seemed a long time before he answered. "I heard it was because of what happened to Señor Scheele."

Watching him, I said: "He was drowned."

He was cautious to the last. "I was told otherwise, señor."

I didn't have a chance to press him. More tables were filling up and he was called away; kept busy for minutes on end. But I had learned enough to want to learn more. The ring was incidental. Overnight and throughout the morning the question-marks about Scheele had worn thin with use, but all at once I sensed there were hints and rumours to be had if I knew where to look for them.

Twice I tried to catch Joaquin's attention. Busy though he was I had the impression that his blindness was deliberate. At long last, as he hurried within earshot, I baited him by ordering another coffee. But before he could bring it I saw Ilsa emerge from the Civil Guard doorway and my pre-occupation was broken. I stood up at once and went to meet her, wondering uneasily to what degree Romero had tainted her grief with regret that she and I had ever met.

CHAPTER SIX

1

I BELIEVE I could have forgiven Romero even the idiocy of his session with Ilsa had I not felt that the very nature of his probing had made him Scheele's ally.

"Has he finished with you?"

"I think so." With a hardness of tone that I was beginning to fear she added: "I hope so."

We walked in silence to the Bar Sinbad. Pigeons scattered, clapping away over the trees. Hardly had we sat down than Joaquin arrived with my coffee. I indicated that it was for Ilsa; ordered another. He was impassively attentive—just another waiter whose world was peopled by strangers, who practised his English and apparently never went to bed.

"Who translated, Ilsa?"

"A man from the Berlitz School." She removed her sunglasses and her eyes confirmed the set of her lips. Confusion, distress, self-reproach—at that moment I read her like a book. I should have known how impossible it is to compete with the dead.

"Was it all about me?" ("Us," I nearly said, but it would have implied no injustice, and injustice was one of the few weapons I thought I had left.)

"Mostly." She accepted a cigarette: shook her head slowly. "I told him again and again that I was with you all that day, but he wouldn't listen. He was like someone hitting a nail into a wall—on and on. It was all so stupid." She clenched her free hand so that the knuckles whitened. "Stupid and cruel."

I said gently: "I warned you, Ilsa."

"He's even had your woman in—"

"Catalina?"

She nodded. "He thinks you gave her a free day on Tuesday for some other reason." She faltered near the end, but finished the sentence. You weren't always ashamed, I thought. But I said: "He's crazy."

"First it was about the trouble here on Monday night; then about Tuesday—where you were, what you did." She couldn't keep the cigarette still. "He isn't interested in Erich. Not really. He is only interested in trying to prove something about you. Erich doesn't matter."

She was bitter, and such was my mood that the complaint seemed not to be levelled against Romero. It wasn't: "Why won't he believe us? Why does he bother himself with you?"—but: "Why did you ever come to blows with Erich? Why did we spend that day as we did?" The true depths of another's grief are impossible to plumb. But I was despairing enough—and therefore sensitive enough—to suspect that it was me she resented. Without me Romero had no power to hurt—and the dead are blameless anyhow; to be murdered is the ultimate injustice. Even so, I said: "I'll give him another twenty-four hours. If he hasn't retracted by then I'm going to my Consulate in Barcelona."

She wasn't really listening. Momentarily exasperated, I thought: You can't live with a ghost. You can't sleep with it, eat with it, talk with it. You betrayed his body when it was yours: why pine for it now?

Joaquin brought the second coffee, slipped the bill-ticket under the saucer with the air of someone leaving a message. I picked it up, turned it over, and the newly-enlisted conspirator in me was put out to find that it bore nothing except the price. Zavella's offer to return the ring hadn't left the surface of my mind, but I had decided to say nothing about it to Ilsa. In her present state the mere mention of it would only have anchored her to Scheele all the more: in any case I wanted to clear the ground of all possibility of disappointment by first having the ring in my possession.

Achievement weighs heavier in the scales than any promise.

We talked spasmodically. Soon we were treading old ground, bogged down amongst the question-marks. It was getting us nowhere and I said as much. For a moment I thought I had hurt her again; added quickly: "You must know I'm right, Ilsa. At least Romero's got a wall to hit his nail into: we haven't got either."

She lifted her chin defiantly.

"It was an accident," I went on. "It *must* have been. A friend of mine—at home, this was—once got some pellets shot into his legs when he was out walking. He could easily have been killed. Mistakes like that *do* happen; dreadful mistakes. ... Either that, or Erich put up a fight when someone tried to rob him. Whoever it was might have panicked and cleared off—or even been caught by the damburst himself. For all we can tell he was killed, too."

Only a couple of hours earlier these had been her own bewildered guesses, but they no longer seemed to satisfy her. They didn't entirely satisfy me either, but I reiterated them now for the same reason that I withheld my information about the ring. I had no remorse; nothing to avenge. But it was conceivable that I might discover something pertinent if I kept my eyes and ears open. Might: I put it no stronger than that. ... One becomes more calculating the harder one fights; more dishonest.

"It's not knowing that's so terrible," she said. "Not being sure."

"Perhaps we'll never know. It's a possibility you've got to face."

"I couldn't bear to think that."

Close-to, I heard a woman say: "That's Stephen Tyler, there—with the blonde. She's the one whose husband—" The voice stopped abruptly when I turned my head. Blue-rinsed hair, spectacles decked with diamante, thin, dissatisfied lips—she hadn't the courage to brazen out the hatred of my look. She dropped her eyes and her face coloured. Meanwhile her companion was still asking:

"Where, Gloria? *Who* did you say? ..."

I wasn't sure whether Ilsa had also heard; desperately hoped she hadn't. But I wasn't mistaken. There was no end to Scheele's allies. Almost immediately, she said, "Let's go, Ty."

"Of course." Then, as we were getting into the car: "What d'you want to do?"

"I just don't want to be in a cage, that's all."

I avoided the coast-road past the villa, the area of the dam, the hills where we had found the waterfall. For once I was scrupulously fair. Sometimes, on the sharper bends, the centrifugal tug pulled us together, dragged us joylessly apart, and I ached for her as much as if she had teased me. The road was white and dusty. To either side, above terraced shelves of red earth, above mottled patches of chestnut and fir, the hills stood bare and crumpled against the sky. An occasional village broke the lower patterns of almond and olive and the bright strips of young green wheat laid between rows of citrus trees. But I was impervious to beauty. Scheele was present in the car as surely as if he rode with us in reality and I knew, without Ilsa having to tell me, that her mind was filled with the dull, wordless images of the past.

It was a week almost to the hour since we had first met and it frightened me to think how small was my claim on her when measured in time and personal knowledge. In the happiness of Monday and Tuesday I had told myself that we would come to learn about each other later, gradually, when it suited us. Passion is self-sufficient. The botanist destroys the flower he dissects: instinctively, I suppose, one shrinks from delving too deeply or too soon. One needs days, weeks—years, even: and Scheele had cut ours short almost as soon as they'd begun. Without effort I could describe the texture of her hair and the feel of her soft, brushing mouth; recall the exact timbre of her laugh, the strength of her small-boned wrists, the intricate whorl of her navel. Dry sherry, paella, filter-cigarettes, black coffee without sugar— I could have made a list of some of her preferences. From Hamburg, about thirty, eight years married, fond of swimming, reasonably read, little travelled. ... After that the enormous blank spaces began. Love is a privileged condition and not an ability to compile a catalogue: yet, jealously, I knew that Scheele would have been able to fill in every gap. Four thousand days against my seven. ...

She rubbed salt into the wound by starting to speak more freely of him. I suppose she was trying to re-shape the old questions; make sense where none existed. But it was hard to take. Once she said: "Erich didn't find friends easily. But he didn't have an enemy in the world—not that kind of enemy." And, later: "He was excited when the Barcelona business came up. He'd never been to Spain. For weeks he had been talking about it and looking at his maps." Each utterance was like the disjointed revelations of a person with fever whose thoughts now and again flow over into words. Why tell me, I thought, unless you deliberately mean to hurt? Do you despise yourself so? Another time she said: "You met him when he was at his worst. We didn't always get along, but he was never in the mood he was here. He seemed to hate everything about Spain when we arrived— why, I don't know. He wouldn't say.' And, finally: "He wasn't always a salesman. Most of his life he was a soldier. I didn't know him then, of course, but I don't think he found it easy to be out of uniform."

What did I care what he was?

I turned for Bandaques at a T-junction. Until then it hadn't dawned on me that we were being followed, but the blue Simca which had quivered in the rear-view mirror for the past quarter of an hour was beginning to make itself a little too obvious. Romero's persistent nonsense angered me and I swore at him under my breath: Haven't you anything better to do? Can't you forget Scheele either?

It was almost one o'clock before the saffron tower of the Church of the Incarnation came into view. When I mentioned food Ilsa protested that she wasn't hungry, but I insisted on her having something. We went to one of the fish restaurants near the amphitheatre where we had not been seen together before. The Simca cruised past while I was trying to park. There were two Civil Guards in it and I sounded my horn at them. Ilsa ate sparingly, immersed in thought. Impossible though it was I longed for one flash of her former self; one renewal of recognition of me. The nearest she came to it was when, as the meal was ending, she said: "You've been a tremendous help, Ty. I don't know what I would have done without you." And somehow it pained me more than if she had remained silent: even if she had looked at me, touched my arm, the acknowledgement wouldn't have seemed so dutifully sterile.

"Tell me what you've decided about the funeral, Ilsa." I was reduced to offering good deeds. "I'll help all I can."

"I will have to see a priest."

"Are you going to have Erich buried here?"

She nodded.

"What about informing your Consul? That may be necessary. In any case he'll be able to advise you."

"I'll ask the priest." Her voice was stone cold. "He will know what I should do."

Without thinking, I said: "But he'll be a Catholic. There isn't—"

"Erich was a Catholic."

"I see." How little I knew: how much of a stranger I was. "Is that what you are, Ilsa?"

"Yes."

I said lamely: "I won't be much help to you there, I'm afraid."

"Perhaps you would take me."

"To the church?"

"Yes."

"Of course. When d'you want to go?"

"As soon as you are ready."

I paid the bill and we left. Whether we were followed again I didn't know—or care. We could have walked, comfortably, but I took the car and sounded my way along a succession of sunless, slot-like streets. Strings of laundry hung across the narrow carriageways: canned music blared from

107

balconied windows. Two days earlier we would have joked about it, pretended that we were part of some triumphant procession, waved at the faces peering down at us. But now we said nothing; looked straight ahead. Scheele was with us still, insisting on being remembered, excluding me with the sheer weight of all the days that I had never shared; labelled in a way that she, and not I, could understand.

The Church of the Incarnation stood on the very edge of the promontory, fronted by a spacious semi-circle of sprinkled lawns. Concrete paths converged on the tiled area in front of the huge west door. Ilsa paused for a moment as we left the car and stared up at the sombre Baroque façade: clouds moved behind the tower so that it seemed to be about to fall. She borrowed a handkerchief and covered her head before we went in. The intense gloom of Spanish churches invariably takes me by surprise. A sepulchral quiet wrapped itself around us: fully half a minute elapsed before either of us could see properly. Shafts of light, stale with incense, leaned in through lofty windows. The interior slowly took shape: small, furtive sounds began to emerge—the soft slap of sandalled feet, a low murmuring, the abacus click of beads. We were not alone. A galaxy of candles burned before the gaudy figure of the Virgen de la Tarde, each flame as firm as a bud in the lifeless air. Her feet were worn by the touch of the superstitious and a man with the face of a Moor knelt in front of her like a slave. Except that his lips moved he might have been taken for another statue, and I remember thinking: You didn't drive them out after all.

The high altar was draped in green; backed by an ornate, carved reredos. Some women were cleaning the floor by the altar rails, above which was suspended an enormous twisted effigy of the crucified Christ. A group of tourists clustered round a guide near one of the side altars; his bored, machinegun monotone reached us like a prayer. In the afternoon they would go to The White Caves; to the Bar Sinbad in the evening. They would have "done" Bandaques by tomorrow and be writing their postcards elsewhere.

Ilsa and I moved down the aisle towards the sanctuary. A priest rounded a pillar by a battery of curtained confessional boxes and I stopped him.

"Can you spare me a moment?"

"Certainly." His chin was as loose-jowled as a turkey's; his eyes weary with sad amazement at the world's indifference. "What is it?"

"This lady's husband was killed the other day and she wants to arrange about his funeral."

He peered. "I see." Death was a commonplace. "She is not Spanish?"

"No."

My manner was obviously alien to him. "Are you a Catholic, señor?"

"The lady is. Her husband was, too. He was killed when the Lareo Dam broke the other day."

"The German?" He read the papers, then; wasn't entombed as one might have supposed.

"That's right. I've come with her because she doesn't—"

"I speak a little German."

He took Ilsa aside; engaged her in question and answer. With my handkerchief knotted under her chin her face was like a child's—trusting and obedient. I was disconcerted by the suddenness with which I had been made an onlooker. An old woman genuflected in front of the altar; blessed herself. Another kissed a candle as if it were a lucky charm and lit it from one of many others that honoured a grotesque saint. A notice on the first of the confessionals announced that the priest whose cubicle it was spoke French and German. There were more notices on some of the other boxes: Polish, I saw: Italian, English. Only if one came from some unlikely extremity could one apparently escape the net.

Interrupting, I said to Ilsa: "Is there anything you'd like me to do?"

"No, thank you, Ty."

"How long will you be?"

"It is difficult to say."

"Shall I wait?"

"You'd better not. I may be some time."

"Where shall I meet you, then? At the España? About six?"

"Yes," she nodded. "Make it at the España."

The priest gestured towards a side door and she went away with him, as close as a prisoner. Everything and everyone was pulling on Scheele's end of the rope. I waited a while, staring about me at the esoteric trappings of faith that could help to bring about my defeat. One mocks, I suppose, out of envy. At any rate, I looked up at the effigy on the cross which presided over the great vault where I stood and, with spite, thought: You, too.

2

It was glaringly bright outside. A beggar came, pleading with a toothless gargoyle grin as I paused when the sun hit me. I bought him off and made for the car before others followed suit. One of the tourists, a Cockney with an open-necked shirt who looked like a boxer, was saying indignantly to a woman: "I warned you, didn't I? It was that Vim rouge with your dinner. It's not like beer, you know."

I hadn't counted on having the afternoon to myself. For a while I thought of returning to the Bar Sinbad and taking up with Joaquin where I had left off. But something he had said earlier in the day gave me another idea: I would go to Gondra. A remembered phrase is sometimes like a key to a code. At the time it may do no more than arouse a mild curiosity, but on reflection one realizes that, without it, one might have continued to puzzle in vain. Joaquin had said: "What is there at Gondra? It was a forgotten place even before the waters came—not even on the maps."

Not even on the maps. ...

Sitting in the car, I checked: as far as mine was concerned he was right. All along I had assumed that sheer chance had taken Scheele to Gondra. I was still ready to think so—

110

until I recalled that he had told Ilsa he was going there; had named it in advance. ... All right, then: he knew it existed. Was that so mysterious? He could have heard of it: his map could have been older than mine. There were several possible explanations and there was no point in wondering which was the most likely. But no harm would come of my following in his tracks. I had three hours to kill. Before long I would probably be able to say: "Ilsa, I've managed to get hold of Erich's ring." If only I could also say: "I've got an idea how he might have died" perhaps it would help to lay his ghost for ever.

Mildly curious, then, I headed in the direction of the Lareo Dam. I left Bandaques by a deliberately circuitous route, not wanting Romero on my tail if he were still that way inclined. A newspaper illustration on the day after the dam's collapse had shown me roughly where Gondra was—or, rather, where its shell had once been. Almost anywhere except in Spain there would have been coach-parties busily ferrying back and forth: the more orderly the way of life, the more morbid is the fascination in disaster. But the road to the dam was totally deserted. *Lo que sera, sera.* There was suffering enough.

It was said locally that God had made the area to the south and west of the town when He had finished shaping the rest of the earth and was tired. The hills reared up, gaunt and barren, burned dry again after the days'-long deluge. Within ten minutes I had entered another world, savagely desolate and deformed. Scheele would have come this way, staring about him, noting, no doubt, the complete absence of trees, the heat-split sandstone bluffs that towered like fortress walls, the dust-green explosions of cactus. Five minutes later a newly-erected board proclaimed that it was prohibited to continue southwards, but I ignored it and went on. Six or seven miles to my left the sea looked as smooth as a sheet of smoked glass: over the same shoulder Bandaques was like a festering scar, all yellows and whites. The road kept going mad, seeking a way to surmount the next ridge, descend the next slope. Bandaques and the sea presently disappeared and I knew that I was getting near. A little further on, I remembered, was a particularly vicious hairpin, after which there was a level run of about a kilometre before I could expect to see any signs of devastation.

I took the hairpin cautiously, in low gear. I was busy straightening out when a Civil Guard stepped into the road from behind a clump of prickly-pear and signalled at me to stop. The following wave of dust drifted over him as he approached the car. He turned his head sideways, screwing his eyes. As it cleared, I said innocently: "What's wrong?"

"Didn't you see the notice back there?" He cleared his throat.

"No."

Then he spat. "You couldn't have missed it."

"I must have done. Either that or I didn't understand what it said."

"You speak Spanish well enough." He wasn't too sure of himself with a foreigner. "Anyway, you'll have to turn back. The road is closed."

"I don't want to go much further."

"You can't, even if it were permitted. It's impossible. Further on there's a hundred metres of nothing." He squinted at me dubiously. "Where are you from?"

"Bandaques."

"Well, then"—which was another way of saying: "You know what happened, so have some sense."

"I'm not going to the dam at all. I'm trying to get to Gondra."

He whistled with surly amusement. "You're even more optimistic than I thought. Anyhow, the answer is still no."

"I have Captain Romero's approval."

His expression changed. "*You* have?"

"Yes."

"In writing?"

"He said it wasn't necessary." The lies came easily; gave me a degree of malicious pleasure. "I have a personal interest in what happened here. Captain Romero suggested that I came out and saw for myself."

"I see," the guard muttered slowly. He glanced round as if wishing he had a companion with whom to confer. "The captain has given his authority?" He wanted to hear me say it again.

"I've told you."

He paused, then took the plunge. "Very well." I felt a little sorry for him. His hands came into play. "Gondra is about two kilometres downstream of the broken dam. There's a side road leading off a couple of hundred metres from where we are now. The junction is a bit overgrown, but you'll hardly miss it. But I doubt if the road exists any more once it drops over into the valley. It's like a pig's trough down there. You won't be able to use your car."

"I'll take it to the junction." I flattered him. "Is that all right?"

"Certainly, señor." The "señor" was an innovation. He stood back; actually smiled. "But rather you than me."

I drove on. Sprouts of cactus flanked the badly-metalled surface. I couldn't remember having seen the fork whenever I had been this way before, but it was easily enough found now that I was looking for it. Presumably Gondra had once been served by a proper road, but all that was left was a double-wheel track with a central hump. I followed it just long enough to get the car out of sight from the highway, then started to walk. The heat bounced off the rocks with implacable intensity and there was a silence that always seems to accompany fierce sunlight. For a time the area of the dam remained hidden from me and only the ragged upper levels of the opposite wall of the valley were visible. But gradually, as the track pointed downwards, the trough began to open up and I had my first glimpses of what the waters had done. My imagination had led me to expect a more dramatic revelation. True, the narrow valley floor was scoured redder than blood; weirdly strewn with boulders and pock-marked with sodden craters. But from high up it was an almost peaceful scene which somehow failed to communicate the sense of vast and fearful violence. Nature has a way of belittling itself; its cataclysms often need some man-made yardstick to give them understandable proportions. And it was only when I saw what remained of the Lareo Dam that I grasped more fully what must have happened when the waters suddenly took over.

Virtually nothing remained of the dam's lofty curve. A huge V, jagged yet curiously symmetrical, had been driven through the massively thick concrete as contemptuously as if it were an egg-shell. The bottom-most point of the V continued to leak a reddish dye on to mounds of smashed masonry. At the top, left and right, I could see the midget silhouettes of men loosely grouped on the out-jutting sections of road: there was a mobile crane up there, too, its arm like a twig against the sky. One thing dwarfed another, giving perspective to the immensity of the forces that had found liberation.

The track continued its gentle descent, slavishly following the contours, and the trench broadened a little. The sickly odour of drying mud began to hang like a vapour on the quivering air. Looking across the valley I could see that a livid stain had been deposited along the rocky slopes—an uneven veneer which in places still glistened. Here and there huge chunks of sandstone had been ripped away, leaving caves like gaping eye-sockets. Sometimes the line of discoloration rose fiercely upwards like a wave, ten or fifteen feet higher than elsewhere: sometimes there were freakish piles of detritus trapped by an outcrop.

Without warning the track disappeared and I found myself shoe-deep in slime. Almost immediately I passed a thrush impaled on a broken cactus spike, and because I imagined it to have been caught in flight by a leaping tongue of water I could picture the terrifying speed at which the flood-head must have thundered seawards. The mud deepened. Twice I slipped; twice nearly quit and returned to the car. But always, at the back of my mind, was the question: What possessed Scheele to come here? Even when the track had been negotiable it could have promised little—a ruin, a barren view; no more. What was so special about a place that was empty and forgotten before the valley was so savagely flushed out? When was it left to rot? And why? Every question bred another. Even so, despite my curiosity, when I slipped a third time I would have given up my quest as a bad job and gone home but for the fact that, as I got to my feet, I saw what could only be Gondra about a quarter of a mile away. It was merged into the blood-red landscape of the side of the valley as surely as if it had been camouflaged: what gave it away was the regularity of its broken outline— an unmistakable geometry of shapes and angles.

I squelched nearer. From the first I had supposed that Gondra was some ancient settlement—Roman, perhaps. The Mediterranean coast of Spain is littered with them and occasionally the Spaniard seemed to grow tired of the less noteworthy, abandoning interest in them for a few generations at a stretch. But this place had no great antiquity; had been just another village. Even the mud couldn't obliterate the character and pattern of what remained. The few thick walls that still stood were those which had been end-on to the flood—here part of a house, there an archway; the outline of a narrow street, a small central square; stumps of pillars which indicated the position of a tiny church. Broken buildings evoke a special kind of melancholy. People had lived here— married, wept, died, prayed, gossiped, copulated, danced; won favours from an unwilling soil. How many people?—two or three hundred? There could hardly have been more. Now a lizard ran like a spurt of green flame: flies swarmed on the carcass of a dead rat. Life somehow always goes on. Mud filled every crevice; swelled the base of every upright. Sometimes it was like walking in glue. Now and again I went in up to my ankles, and each sucking step seemed to release its quota of trapped stench. I could have kicked myself for coming: all I had done was to ruin a pair of shoes and foul my clothes. Scheele's Mercedes had been found some distance further on, so it was probable that he had driven this far: yet, for all I knew, he had also felt like kicking himself as he

115

wandered in disappointment through the desolation. And then what had happened? I was no nearer to an answer. If there were any clues in Gondra they were inches deep in slime or, like Scheele, had been swept away. Mine weren't the only footprints: others had been here before me—search parties, soldiers, the Civil Guard; God knows who. I was wasting my time.

After some minutes I couldn't stand the smell any longer. I was in what I imagined had been the square. Two or three shattered sections of wall—none of them more than shoulder-high—still remained. The framework of what might have been a communal well was silted right over so that it looked like a lump of raw material on a potter's wheel. I plodded past it, stumbling on a hidden rock, feeling the warm wet stickiness seeping inside my shoes. One of the bespattered walls was plastered a greenish blue and had something written on it—or at least I thought it was writing. I noticed it quite by accident. Curiosity dies hard: I took a stick and scraped the thin coating of mud away. R, I saw, then RÁ, then RÁN. The black paint had worn pale with age, but was still quite clear. I worked to the left, using the stick with both hands, PASARÁN ... NO PASARÁN. There was nothing in front of the first N. With some excitement I moved to the right and scraped again. The defiant phrase was repeated— NO PASARÁN, except that the stonework splintered to an end across the last letter. My hands might have been bleeding as I stood back and looked at the faded slogans which had survived sun and wind and rain and flood. There had been no need to uncover the repetition. As soon as the two words were readable I had known approximately how long they had been there and when Gondra had died. No one in Spain had scrawled THEY WILL NOT PASS for more than twenty years.

I scraped lower, nearer the base of the wall, and a second phrase slowly gave itself up. TODO O NADA. ... ALL OR NOTHING. I felt the sadness of the place as never before. All or nothing. ... For whoever had lived here it had been nothing.

Nothing. *Nada.* ...

It was as if a light came on in my mind. *Nada.* ... All at once I remembered Scheele in the Bar Sinbad on the night before he was to die. *"Nada,"* the whisky had made him say. "For them it was *nada.*" And there and then suspicion was born in me that he had been to Gondra more than once.

3

The Civil Guard on the road grinned when he saw me. "I warned you, señor. Was it worth it?"

"I think so."

I drove towards Bandaques, strangely elated. At the first hotel I came to I stopped and went in. The man at the reception desk glanced at my shoes and trouser-legs with undisguised disapproval.

"D'you understand German?"

He gave a prompt, if unimpressive, sample. *"Ja wohl."*

"I don't, so I'd appreciate your help. ... I may have got this wrong. Can you tell me what is the meaning of '*hier haben wir wonnen*'?"

"Hier haben wir wonnen?"

"Something like that."

"Wonnen," he muttered. *"Wonnen...* Are you certain the last word is '*wonnen*'?"

"I'm not certain about any of it."

"Wonne?" he offered. "No, it couldn't be..." Then he snapped his fingers. *"Gewonnen.* Could you mean '*hier haben wir gewonnen*'?"

"Possibly. What's that in Spanish?"

"We won here."

It made electrifying sense. "We won here?"

"That's right. But—"

"We won here," I repeated; paused for a moment while it sank in. Then: "I'm very grateful."

He was baffled. "I don't understand, señor—"

"A friend of mine asked me to inquire," I laughed off the explanation. "Don't ask me why. Thank you again."

Memory is rarely flawless or obliging: that afternoon mine was both. Names frequently escape me within minutes of my hearing them, and I have sometimes searched all day for an elusive word. Yet on the slushy trudge out of the valley I recalled *"hier haben wir gewonnen"* without effort and with passable accuracy. Scheele had murmured it the evening we first met, when his anger over the theft had been damped down and his speech had become slurred. "They forget," he'd said. Then, confidentially: *"Hier haben wir gewonnen."*

"We won here ..." His unending contempt at last took on meaning. Obedience, authority, respect—"we had it once." On the hateful night after his visit to Barcelona his complaint was: "I've been dealing with little men; men without memories. Some people don't mind humiliating themselves, but I am not that kind—least of all here." To have been the victor and no longer to be acknowledged; to be reduced to bargaining with the vanquished—this was what had galled him. He had returned to find that the one monument which stood amid the ruins of his own subsequent defeat had never even been erected. He was a typewriter salesman, a tourist; nothing more. I could remember a score of remarks he had made which, at the time, were unintelligible. He wasn't an object of study then and I had not bothered with them, but now I understood their significance. One triggered off another. And it wasn't only what he had said. ... On our visit to the archaeological museum there had been a couple of show-cases which, with true Spanish incongruity, were devoted to local relics of the Civil War—a charred bible, a miscellany of buttons, bullets and badges, a printed proclamation or two, some fragments of shell. It was a trivial collection but Scheele had given it the same keen attention as everything else—keener, even. In particular he had removed his dark glasses to peer at a yellowed card which identified some jagged shrapnel splinters and shaken his head critically as if he had once more found fault with something. Again, at the time, I had not been sufficiently interested. Now, armed with new knowledge, I realized that it must have been the numerals which had attracted him—probable the calibration details—because he couldn't read Spanish.

I drove home and changed. I had done no more than piece a few half-facts together but I believed I was forging a weapon which I could use on Ilsa. I was quite certain that she was ignorant of what I had discovered. Her bewilderment was absolutely genuine. Scheele had been here before but she didn't know it; couldn't explain his mood. "A soldier once, before I knew him." Everything fitted, given the first fluky clue. ... I wasn't concerned with who had murdered him; that was Romero's business. But if I couldn't lay his ghost perhaps I could expose it.

It was nearly half-past five. I called in at the Bar Sinbad on my way to the España and spoke to Joaquin. He wasn't busy. I led off in his own tongue to forestall a confusing excursion into English.

"What exactly happened at Gondra, Joaquin?"

"The flood, d'you mean?"

"The other time."

He lifted his shoulders. "It was a long while ago."

"About 1938?"

"It is best forgotten."

"Remember for a moment."

"The place was destroyed."

"In the fighting?"

"People do not talk about it any more, Señor Tyler."

"Was it that bad?"

"The whole war was bad."

"Who destroyed Gondra?"

"The same people who destroyed Spain. But what does it matter now? It was done. Nothing will be changed by thinking about it. We have an old saying: Today's dust is foul enough... D'you understand me?"

I nodded. "Tell me something else."

"Of course."

"Were you there?" He would have been about twenty-five then.

"No, thank God. There are very few left who were. The rest—" He let a gesture finish for him.

"The women, too?"

"Everyone, señor. Everyone."

Nobody called him but he walked away; flicked his cloth over some empty tables. I had never seen him moved before. A fish-seller pushed a barrow along the street, blowing a conch shell, and the mournful sound sent the pigeons clapping through the plane trees. Romero emerged from the Civil Guard building and was driven off in his official car. I would get my apology yet—as a bonus. Keep on being blind, I thought. Keep on being stupid.

Joaquin returned. "I am seeing Luis tomorrow about the ring."

"So soon?"

"I will let you have it when you are next here."

"Does he come to you, or is it the other way round?"

"I go to him."

Something urged me to say: "I'd like to accompany you." Zavella's quixotic offer had intrigued me from the first. I suppose it was this that prompted me.

When Joaquin realized I was serious he frowned slightly. "Luis might not want anything like that."

"He's in my debt. It's not much to ask."

He thought for a while, pursing his lips, torn between loyalties. "It would be inconvenient for you, Señor Tyler. Very early in the morning, a long walk, a hard climb. ... It would be better if you got the ring from me here."

"I could pick you up in my car. That would save—"

"No." He was quite sharp. "You would be followed."

"Would be, or have been?"

"Both."

Nothing much escaped him. "I wasn't followed this afternoon," I said.

"They are not always clever. But it would be a risk."

"All right: no car. How, then?"

He sighed. "You are insisting, aren't you, señor?"

"No. Just asking. Between friends."

"Luis will probably never forgive me."

"You make me sound like an enemy."

There was no one near but Joaquin spoke more quietly. "Take the bus which runs to The White Caves—the first bus in the morning from the amphitheatre. It goes at half-past six. Buy a five peseta ride. Go as far as the bridge below the caves."

"And then?"

"I will show you."

"We meet there?" I was an amateur.

"No—I'll be on the bus. But in case we can't sit together it will look better if you know where to get off. I will go on to another stop, then walk back."

"What time will we return to Bandaques?"

"About ten."

"That'll be fine." Already, I felt, he was regretting the arrangement and I thought it best to leave before he changed his mind. "Don't let me down, will you?"

"No, Señor Tyler." As I got up he said: "Why are you so anxious to meet Luis?"

I fobbed him off. "Why does a writer do anything, Joaquin? You ought to know me by now."

The sun was pushing long level rays over the rooftops as I walked into the España. Ilsa was waiting for me in the American Bar.

"Did you get anything arranged?"

"For Saturday," she said. "Saturday morning at eleven."

"Was the priest helpful?"

"He couldn't have been kinder."

We were as polite as if it were a first meeting. She'd received a cable from Scheele's firm offering condolences and assistance: also one from her father.

I paraded my ignorance. "Is he in Hamburg, too?"

"In Munich."

I had made love to her, but others knew the detailed framework of her life: I was on hand, but others were breaking up my monopoly.

She asked: "Where were you this afternoon?"

"Nowhere in particular. I just filled in time."

I had never lied to her before. I longed for her body but to win it I would have to destroy the image in her mind. But not yet; not yet. I wanted the weapon perfected first.

Love, as I knew it that afternoon, had never heard of compassion.

CHAPTER SEVEN

THE INTERIOR of the bus reeked with an accumulation of exhaled garlic. I was one of the first to climb aboard. There were ten minutes to spare and I yawned, shivering slightly, out of touch with so early an hour. I had slept badly; after four scarcely at all. At one time I had come close to changing my mind about wanting to meet Zavella. What did I expect to learn? A quixotic gesture loses its curiosity value when one frets for sleep. But in the hour or so before dawn, when there was clearly no more sleep to be found, I had listened to the turgid pulse of the sea and concentrated my thoughts upon Scheele. What little I had discovered about him had been virtually handed me on a plate: if I wanted more I would have to go looking for it. And I did want more: I wanted a glimpse of whatever it was that had lingered in his memory over so long a period. Joaquin was my only useful contact in Bandaques but I doubted if he could provide me with anything more than background. Scheele had sat unrecognized at his tables; been judged, like any tourist, on the standard of his tipping. He knew a good deal of what went on locally, had his contacts, and presumably fed Zavella with news and gossip from time to time. But somebody who lived by his wits would almost certainly have more sources of information than one. At least, that was what I had convinced myself as the greyness of approaching dawn began to filter into the air. I would go: nothing would be lost by it.

The bus filled slowly. Almost without exception the passengers were men—shabby in faded dungarees and patched corduroy. I guessed most of them to be labourers at the tobacco factory being built to the north-west of the town: constant exposure to a harsh sun and the resignation that comes of fifty pesetas a day had lined the faces of even the youngest of them. I sat and waited for Joaquin, wondering whether he would acknowledge me or not; then, as time passed, whether he was going to break his promise after all. But a minute before the half hour he clambered in and came to the vacant seat beside me. I had never seen him without white jacket and black tie: he still wore the braided trousers—presumably to facilitate a quick change on his return—but the open-necked shirt and black beret somehow destroyed the El Greco mould of his features. He looked a fraction less pale; less drawn.

In English he said: "That chair is available, señor?"

I indicated assent and he sat down. He had a small brown paper packet with him, tied with string, and might have been a guide on his way to the day's stint at The White Caves. A series of glances round the bus seemed to satisfy him that English gave us complete security.

"Were you followed?"

"Followed? Not that I know of: I walked along the beach. What have you got there?"

"Food."

"You ought to have brought your Wordsworth."

He wasn't in a smiling mood. "I think I will be in trouble about this."

"I'll explain. Don't worry."

He shrugged.

"How long's the ride?"

"Twenty minutes."

The driver and ticket-collector stamped out their cigarettes and left the amphitheatre wall. There was a muttered chorus of greeting from some of the regulars. Doors slammed, the engine fired and we lurched away, the horn blaring as stridently as if the streets had been solid with traffic. Soon we were on the main highway to the northwest; the fringes of the town running squalidly to seed among fig and locust trees. Dawn had come with a bloody froth of cloud. Now the sky was at peace, the colour not yet burned out of it, and one bright abandoned star glittered coolly above the blue mist shrouding the sierras.

Ilsa would still be asleep. The thought of her was as potent and disturbing as ever, but the yearning had lost its simplicity; was undermined with doubts, growing vindictive. Why else was I sitting here with a waiter from the Bar Sinbad? Not because of the ring and whatever merit I had once thought its recovery might earn me. And not in the hope of eventually being able to ease her mind about the manner of Scheele's death. She wasn't alone in having changed: only in desire had I remained constant.

Joaquin and I bought our tickets separately. The collector joked crudely with the pair behind us and a woman across the gangway laughed. The sun flooded warmly in. Every so often the bus stopped to pick someone or other up. Before long there were as many passengers standing as there were sitting and the springs groaned ominously as we rattled over the worst stretches of pot-holes. But at the site of the new factory there was an almost complete exodus and we were left with about half a dozen people for company.

"Do you always come by bus?"

Joaquin said: "It depends where I have to go."

"It varies?"

"Again, please."

"There's more than one place?"

"There are several places. But I never go twice like the last time—you understand?" Presently, he added: "You are doing something not many ever done, Mister Tyler."

It still troubled him, but I found it hard to believe that I was a conspirator: the fact that we had to raise our voices to compete with the rattle and crunch of the bus didn't help.

"Do others go sometimes?"

"I believe."

"Who?"

"Friends."

"What about his family? Don't they ever see him?"

"There is only me."

"No brothers or sisters?"

"He never has these. Me, though—and friends. He has many friends." There was an odd note of pride in his voice.

The road was burrowing into the hills. We stopped at a village. An old man got in carrying a live rabbit: its legs were trussed and he pushed it on to the overhead rack from where it looked down at me with eyes huge with terror. A black dog, all skin and bone, yelped at the bus deliriously as it ground away.

I asked: "How long's he lived like this?"

"Most his life."

"Why? What started it?"

"Ask him, Mister Tyler, not me."

"Did he kill someone?"

"Luis? Never! He has done bad things since, but these are to live. Smuggling, stealing—"

"And he's never been caught?"

"Please?"

"Captured?" I leaned a fraction closer. *"Un preso?"*

"Ah. ... Once—two years ago. In a village over there"—he pointed vaguely. "But he is free before Captain Romero arrives." As if against his will his mouth shaped a smile. "The captain will never forgive him because already he send a message to his chief and it makes him look a fool."

The rabbit eyed me through the quivering slats of the rack. Nothing lasted—freedom no more than anything else: only death was permanent.

"Has he always been near Bandaques?"

"No. After the war, yes: but later, for a long time, he was somewhere different—where I could not say exactly. Albacete, I think: then Calatayud. Now he is here again for six, seven years. Eight, maybe."

The bus shuddered up a twisting incline. A few thinning scarves of mist hung stubbornly below the slag-tip skyline. I looked at my watch: we had been on the move for over a quarter of an hour. The bridge Joaquin had mentioned wasn't all that far away. A Civil Guard suddenly overtook us on a red and black motor-cycle. Joaquin and I exchanged glances: he was tight-lipped, anxious, even when the motorcycle had accelerated out of our sight.

He said urgently: "If he is at the bridge do not get out."

I nodded.

"Stay here—in bus." It was a command.

"Very well."

We stopped outside a ruined house and the old man hauled the rabbit off the rack and lowered himself carefully on to the road. A tile set into one of the pillars of the gate bore the legend: GOD PROTECTS. The conductor leaned out and bawled: "Why not take the strings off its legs and race it home?"

I had been watching for the house. The bridge was a couple of steep turns further on, another minute, but it seemed longer before it slid into view. There was no one to be seen and I signalled the conductor that this was where I wanted.

"One for the bridge, Paco," he called to his gaunt companion at the wheel. "One gentleman tired of life."

He was very pleased with himself but nobody else laughed. I squeezed past Joaquin's bony knees and dropped out on to the verge about fifty yards short of the bridge. The driver crashed into gear and the bus trundled off, spewing dust and fumes. As a precaution I left the road as quickly as possible, hauling myself up the high bank; found a place to wait among some thorn bushes. A great tide of quiet flowed in as the sound of the bus diminished; the air was wonderfully clean after the concentration of garlic and rough cigarette-smoke. The bridge spanned a deep gorge. I could see neither from where I sat, but in the other direction a fawn-grey encrustation on the olive and terracotta landscape below marked a distant village. I thought I heard the bus stop and start up again, but my hearing was urban, unattuned. Before long, though, Joaquin's gritty step was unmistakable and I got to my feet; whistled him. He came up the bank with unexpected agility.

I said in Spanish: "So far, so good."

"That guard had me worried." His eyes wandered over the

hills behind my back.

"He looked to me as if he'd got something else on his mind."

"You never know." He hadn't relaxed one bit.

"Where do we go from here?"

"Follow me."

He led off up the slope. There was low scrub and loose shale; an occasional stunted tree bent by winds which, that morning, refrained. Everything was quite still and a light dew glistened in the flawless sunshine. Sometimes there was a narrow track, sometimes not. The gorge was visible for a time and when I last saw the bridge it looked like a thin plank laid across a series of toy trestles. We climbed without pause for the best part of half an hour until I was forced to call a halt. Sweating, I stood with hands on hips, sucking in lungfuls of burning air.

"I told you what it would be like," Joaquin said. To my shame he was scarcely out of breath. Zavella's reaction to my coming was very much on his mind and I could almost sense him willing me to decide against going further.

"How much more?"

"About the same again."

I moistened my lips and spat. "I expect I'll survive."

We went on. Mercifully the gradients eased a little and we no longer climbed every step of the way. Once over the first ridge Joaquin followed a more switchback course. For some distance we traversed a long belt of conifers: later we were in the open again, moving over ground ribbed with the exposed ends of tilted rock strata. As far as I could tell we were heading south or south-east but I had no clear sense of direction; matching my pace with Joaquin's had me fully occupied. I said to him once: "How in God's name do you and your cousin keep in touch?" Bandaques had begun to seem impossibly remote and I was reflecting on the apparent ease with which information passed between them. But the only answer I received was a grunt. Perhaps he'd decided I'd learned enough as it was: perhaps I was being deliberately confused about our destination. If that were so I had no right to quibble, but there were moments when the strain brought me near to charging him with choosing the longest and most difficult route.

We came at last to a stony plateau which looked as if it had been bombarded by meteorites. There was a scattering of umbrella pines and a great deal of knee-high scrub.

"Wait here, please," Joaquin said uneasily.

I was glad to agree. He walked away under the trees and I found a boulder to lean against; lit a cigarette. The view towards the narrow coastal plain was magnificent. Bandaques was hidden but the sea provided a taut, cobalt skyline. Ridged and furrowed, the hills fell chaotically away, trapping their own shadows. A stream showed in a dark cleft, the village I had seen earlier, a few isolated farmhouses. To my surprise one or two string-like twists of the-road were also visible. Height and broken country combine to deceive, but we were nearer to it than I had imagined. Yet, even if I had wanted to, I doubted whether I could have found my way back to the plateau unaided, or even indicated its approximate whereabouts from below. Intentionally or not, Joaquin had done his work well.

A faint breeze came and went, cool on my sweat. I was alone long enough for the cigarette to burn down to the filter. Then I saw Joaquin moving towards me through the pines. He stopped and indicated that I was to join him. "It's all right," he said as I came up, and I slapped him on the shoulders, glad for his sake, gratitude coming to a belated head.

There were no paths, no hint that we were not the first to walk here. We picked our way through the scrub. The ground was pock-marked with innumerable circular depressions, some small, some large and deep enough to have held a horse and cart. When I caught sight of him Zavella was standing on the lip of one of these, a rifle cradled loosely in his arms. He advanced to meet me, smiling, thrusting out a hand in greeting. The smile I remembered, the slightly hooked nose, the sunken cheeks, the sickly pallor beneath the swarthy skin. But the strength of the sinewy grip I had forgotten; perhaps never noticed the whiteness of his small, even teeth.

"I haven't got a front door, Señor Tyler, and this is no fancy cigarette-lighter. But you're welcome."

"I all but blackmailed Joaquin into this."

"Whatever Joaquin does is all right with me."

"You wouldn't have thought so earlier. He's been like someone waiting for a jury to come back. However, if it's any consolation he's taken me half way round the world since we left the bus."

"He needn't have bothered—not with you."

One end of the depression was roofed over with pine branches which hadn't long been cut. My first glance took in the remains of a fire, a blackened aluminium mug, plucked feathers, a rusty knife, some shreds of broken earthenware, a rolled, coarse blanket. The packet Joaquin had brought with him lay opened on an upturned enamel bowl: some of the bread and meat it contained had already been sampled.

Zavella dropped into the shallow pit. "Come in," he said with self-mockery. Then, to Joaquin: "Are you getting the bus at the half-hour?"

"I must, Luis."

"And you, señor?" Zavella looked at me.

"I'll go with Joaquin."

Joaquin said: "It will be necessary to start back in about thirty minutes."

Zavella reached for meat and bread; filled his mouth. High summer though it was it would have been cold here at night. I looked again at his pitiful collection of belongings; at the gun placed within easy reach. It was hard to think of him as a man with friends. A falling cone dribbled through the branches of a nearby tree: it made an erratic, swishing sound and I saw him start, then relax, before I had even identified it.

About the last thing I expected him to say was: "How is the señora?"

"Well—considering."

He nodded; coughed. I remembered the cough, too, but it

sounded less terrible in the open "She is very beautiful. One of the most beautiful women I have ever seen."

"I didn't know you had."

"Once," he said. He fished into his right-hand trousers' pocket, produced a heavy gold signet-ring and held it up between thumb and bruise-blackened finger-nail. "When I came by this. She was asleep on the bed."

I put out a hand but Zavella's fingers closed; withdrew.

I said: "Nobody could understand how you got in that afternoon."

"Over the roof and down a pipe."

"No key? No help from someone on the hotel staff?"

"What I do I do alone." There was more hardness than swagger.

"Joaquin tells me you sold the other things—the watch and the lighter."

"For very little."

"Yet you're prepared to return the ring?"

"Yes."

"Why, Zavella? That's the main reason I've come—to find out."

Joaquin had sauntered away, leaving us alone. I suppose he was underlining his point that this wasn't really his affair.

"Why?" I asked again.

Zavella tore some bread apart; munched hungrily. He evaded my question by posing his own. "Is the señora aware of the ring?"

"Not yet."

"You wanted to be sure it existed first—am I right?"

"Just about."

His knowing smile stopped as swiftly as it had formed. He produced the ring again, like a conjurer; juggled it from one hand to another. "She will appreciate having it?"

"I imagine so."

"As a keepsake?"

The word disturbed me. "It belonged to her husband."

"She is too young to have been with him long."

131

"They were married eight years. She's distressed, naturally." I couldn't fathom his cat-and-mouse mood, but I bore with it.

"Why should she grieve at all?"

I frowned.

"Why should she grieve when she has you?"

As easily as I could I said: "Joaquin talks too much."

"You would not be here otherwise."

"Nonsense. I came of my own free will."

"Only because you knew I had this." The ring went back and forth, back and forth.

"True," I conceded.

"And I only let you know of it because of what Joaquin had said."

"Which was?"

"That she had finished with him."

A butterfly chopped past. We stared at each other as intently as if a crucial card had been thrown. Vanity always takes precedence, however fleetingly. The truth was practically under my nose but it was obscured by the thought that Zavella was prompted by some romantic streak: the lonelier a man, the more fanciful his imagination.

"Was that so?" he pressed.

I had two choices—"Yes," or "No": either was riddled with doubt. "Yes," I said, and the half-lie twisted in me like a knife.

"That is all I wanted to be sure of. ... Here—catch."

The cough racked him as he tossed the ring at me. It was warm from his touch. I turned it over in my fingers; looked at the square piece of onyx embedded into the gold swelling. ES was engraved fancifully across the mottled green and black surface. It was Scheele's ring, right enough.

Zavella seemed to read my mind. "There's no mistake, Señor Tyler. It was his. Nobody else's."

I was thinking about Ilsa and was deaf to the concentrated loathing in his voice. "I can see that."

"The 'S'"—he paused for maximum effect—"stands for Schafer."

I glanced up.

"His name was Schafer."

"Scheele," I corrected. "Erich Scheele."

"Schafer," he insisted. "I'm talking about his real name. Twenty years ago it was Schafer."

"Twenty *years* ago?"

He nodded. "When I first knew him."

The moment of revelation often comes more quietly than a novelist would sometimes have his readers believe. For me, that morning, there was no blinding flash; no abrupt, astonished reaction. I don't think I even moved. I remember staring at Zavella, elbows on knees, the ring pressed between my finger-tips, and feeling the back of my neck prickle almost as if I were afraid. *You* killed him. It was you, then. ... In the blink of an eye the puzzle had fitted into shape but I was incapable of grasping that it was finished. The answers were almost all there but acceptance of them took seconds to dawn.

Eventually I heard myself say: "That was at Gondra, wasn't it?"

"Yes, that's where." (I recalled from our other meeting: "A boy once. Long ago.")

He stood up. Joaquin took it as a hint. "Can we leave now?"

Zavella glanced at me: "D'you want to go?"

I shook my head; heard Joaquin remark that though we still had ten minutes or so to spare he didn't want to cut it too fine.

Zavella said: "There's a bus every hour. Why not wait for the next?"

"I'm on duty at ten," Joaquin replied, coming across. "You know that."

"Go on your own then. I'll put Señor Tyler on the way to the road when the time comes."

Joaquin hesitated. "Would that be all right?" he asked me. "I can't risk being late."

"Of course." I would have agreed to anything as long as it meant that I stayed.

133

"Is something the matter?" he looked at us both anxiously.

"Nothing. Don't always worry so." With a gesture of affection Zavella took him by the arm. "Good-bye and thanks. Get on back to your tables, *amigo mio,* and come and see me again soon. On Monday, if you can."

"Here?"

"Above the caves."

Joaquin nodded. "Good-bye, señor."

"Good-bye."

Zavella and I watched him walk away, noiseless on the pine needles. When he was nearly lost to view, I said: "Does he know?"

"As far as he is concerned it is just a ring and I am just a thief with a troublesome conscience."

"But he knows about Gondra."

"Everybody does. They know about Guernica, too, but only if you were there does it live with you." He straightened himself, hands on hips. "I hope he never learns more. He is ignorant of what it's like to hate and might not understand what I have done."

"Yet you tell me."

"Because you're involved. Because you're entitled to know what manner of man the señora grieves for. He was your enemy, too, remember."

Was? The tense jarred.

A small bird flipped overhead, emphasizing the silence; our isolation.

I said: "When you broke into his room that day at the España—were you aware who occupied it?"

"Not until later. The señora shifted in her sleep just as I reached the dressing-table. What with that and the shower running in the bathroom I decided it was best to be quick. I scooped up the first things I saw and got out. I was clear of Bandaques before I discovered what a haul I'd made." He coughed dryly. "A long time ago I used to pray that something like it would happen, but prayers such as mine were then are never answered—not by God, anyhow. It was chance. I sweat sometimes when I think of it. I could easily have picked another hotel; another veranda. His happened to be the nearest to the pipe."

I studied the ring as I listened. Schafer. Erich Schafer. ... Ilsa Scheele. ...

Zavella continued: "I found out whose room it was. The name didn't confuse me. The ring was as good as a fingerprint. On the Saturday I came back into the town. I'd tried the day before but there were too many guards about. But on the Saturday, with the crowds, it was easier. I was sure he would be there, somewhere, watching the procession, but one of the guards spotted me and I had to run for it. On the Sunday I heard about you and the señora and about his visit to Barcelona next morning."

(Joaquin, I thought.)

"I hoped to intercept the Mercedes on the road, but somehow I missed it. Then, on the Tuesday, he went to Gondra—as you know. I wasn't here then. I was in another place, near the dam. That was chance, too. I saw his car when it was still a long way away. It was heading for the dam but something told me he would branch off and go to the village. I went down into the valley and waited in the old square. And, sure enough, he came. They say they always come back. He'd changed, of course—gone bald, got fatter. Elsewhere, he might have passed me by unrecognized. But the ring and the fact that he'd returned to Gondra condemned him. He didn't see me in the square at first. Then I called him by name—'Schafer'. He was walking away from me and stopped as if he were tied to a rope which would suddenly let him go no further. He looked to either side. 'Schafer', I called again and he swung round; saw me and the gun I had. He said something I didn't understand. I called: 'I'm the boy who stood here twenty years ago—remember?' I didn't know whether he'd learned Spanish or not but it was unimportant because I thought I had all the time in the world. Then, as I started towards him, the dam broke—and suddenly there was no time at all. Neither of us grasped what had happened—not immediately. It sounded like an underground explosion—muffled, yet violent. There was deathly quiet for a moment or two afterwards, but soon the earth began to shake and a moan came down the valley, louder every second, growing into a roar. It was like a wind, yet the air was dead. All at once Schafer began to run and I shot him, thinking he was running from me. He went down on to his knees and started to scream. Then I saw the water boiling round the bend above the village and I was sure that I was finished, too. It was as high as a cathedral and coming fast, pouring over itself. I threw the gun away and made for the steep ground. I never thought I'd get clear. In the end I had no more than my own length to spare. When I looked back Schafer had gone—everything had gone. I was sick with terror—physically sick: and yet I felt wonderful." He began to cough again. "Wonderful."

He had spoken in a flat, unemotional monotone, as if he were anxious to unburden himself, and the very simplicity of his phrasing made the scene all the more vivid. Gondra I had seen, and the currents had brought Scheele's horror-struck expression almost to my own door. Only when he concluded did his tone change, and then it was viciously triumphant; the final repetition ugly and frightening.

I studied his strained, cadaverous face. "Would you have shot him anyhow?"

"More than once."

"For what reason?"

Zavella swallowed; stirred the fire's dead embers with a worn boot.

"Tell me," I said. "It's important."

It came again like a spate. "The valley was the main defence line for Bandaques and the road to the north. Once it was lost the town and the road were open. This had been recognized for some time. But things had gone badly and the front had moved at great speed—so much so that Gondra hadn't been properly evacuated when the fight for the valley began. It lasted two days and was bitter. Before the war my father worked with explosives for a construction company—he wasn't in the army because he'd lost three fingers from his right hand. But he fought then. When the situation had become almost hopeless he led a group of milicianos upstream to try and blow the dam. They hadn't a chance in a hundred and those who weren't killed were captured—my father among them. They were taken in front of an officer of the Condor Legion who was in command and asked where they came from. Next day, when the valley was lost, they were marched into the square. About a hundred people were still in the village. They were herded out of cellars and basements—old people mainly, though not all. My mother was one and I was another. We were lined up against a wall with the men from the dam, two deep. I was in the front row with my mother. Through an interpreter the officer ordered me away from the rest and made me stand beside him. He was slim, sandy-haired, and smoked a cigarette. I came up to his waist. He stood with his left hand hooked into his belt and there was a ring on the small finger. I was close enough to see the initials. I thought he was going to make a speech. Everyone lining the wall was very quiet and I suppose they thought so too. Like me, I can't believe they knew they were going to be killed. But they were—every single one. Without any warning, without explanation. The officer suddenly lifted his hand and machine-guns opened fire from two corners of the square." Zavella paused, lifting his chin as if he were suffocating. "It was all over in a minute, then some men started cleaning up with rifles and revolvers. The officer got the interpreter to say to me: 'That's what happens if you resist. Now go and warn them in Bandaques.' Then he walked away. He was still smoking. Later he put his guns on the village and flattened it."

Again, by sparing the details, he allowed my imagination every scope. The lapse of time since these things had happened was no barrier. "Obedience, authority, respect"—Scheele's phrase added its counterpoint to my revulsion.

Zavella said: "The interpreter called him Schafer. And he

answered to the name the other day, even if he had changed it to Scheele." He pecked his head towards the ring turning in my fingers. "That was the same, though. That was what led me back to him."

"How old were you?"

"Twelve."

It wouldn't have been fair to tax him, but it was impossible to deny myself a few last questions. "What made him pick you out?"

"I've asked myself a thousand times."

"Were other children there?"

"A few. Babies, mostly. Some of the men tried to break away when the shooting started, but only three or four managed it. They've died since; either that or they've gone somewhere else. In any case I was the only one to hear the officer's name and see the ring close-to. Believe me, Señor Tyler, those initials burned themselves into my brain."

"Did you go to Bandaques?"

"No. I went and hid in a cave. It's hard to remember exactly. I was petrified. Deep down I was hysterical yet I couldn't even cry. A woman found me and took me to her house: fed me. That wasn't the same day—it was the next or the one following: God knows. I think she must have guessed where I was from but she said nothing about it—only fed me and gave me a place to sleep. I believe she was intending to hand me over to some nuns but it didn't come to that because I left the house in the second night and never went back. I just wandered. I was able to cry by then. The fighting had gone north and everything was chaotic. I was too young to realize that it would have been better if I had been killed, too. I don't know where I went. I scrounged when I wasn't taken pity on. For a few days I was with gipsies; later with a family who had a saw-mill. Then, about two weeks after the shooting, I found a live grenade. It was in a ditch where I was collecting berries. The feel of it in my hand somehow thawed the numbness out of me—it's difficult to put it into words. But there and then I seemed to grow up. Tears weren't enough. I waited on a bluff overhanging a road and threw the grenade on the first staff car that passed along north. It missed, but men got out of the car and I was fired at; had to run." The cough bent him over. When it eased, he produced a grim smile. "I've never stopped running since, señor. And it's too late now to hope that I could."

A gold-rimmed cloud was dragging over the sun. The weapon I had sought was forged and ready for use. It was more damaging than anything I had ever visualized and yet it scared me, almost as if I feared that it could also bring about my own destruction.

Zavella said: "Spain was like a slaughterhouse when I wanted to talk about Gondra. Everyone had had his bellyful of death—and there was still more to come. So, after a while, I kept what I knew to myself and learned to live with it. It ate me out like a cancer, though. Even when there was no pain it was always there, gnawing away in secret—five, ten, twenty years afterwards." He lifted his arms away from his body: let them drop. "And now it's all over. A name, a ring, a pipe from a hotel roof—there are miracles to this day."

He led me down from the plateau until I was close enough to the road to be able to continue alone. The last time we parted I had told him that I wasn't sorry for him, but now I was filled with pity. I could neither blame nor judge him. Nothing had gone right for me since Scheele had died and desperation had warped my passion for Ilsa out of recognition. I told myself that Scheele would probably have been killed anyway, bullet or no. Fate is a ruthless redeemer and rarely makes mistakes. Watching Zavella's scarecrow figure ahead of me on the descent I wondered how it would eventually end for him; whether he would find laughter first and know the peace of a woman's body without always straining his senses for the sound of footsteps furtively closing in. Perhaps I wished him these things especially because I had also been deprived of them and inherited a cancerous ache of my own.

As we shook hands, I said: "Maybe we'll meet again."

"I hope so."

"Good luck anyhow. And many years."

"And to you, Señor Tyler."

Twenty minutes later I stopped the bus near the gorge. I saw no guards, no cruising Simca, either while I waited or when I was in the bus. The sun had come out again and the countryside was deceptively tranquil as we left the rough brown folds of the hills and rattled in towards Bandaques. It was just eleven o'clock when I climbed out under the bullfight posters plastered along the amphitheatre wall and started walking to the España.

CHAPTER EIGHT

1

Ilsa wasn't at the hotel and the girl at the reception-desk was no help. I went into the American Bar and drank a Fundador. A man sitting under the mounted head of the bull with the chromium-plated legend was avidly reading the football reports. The bar-tender hadn't seen Ilsa either but he had noticed the juxtaposition of the man and the bull and grinned at me. "Things change," he said, and because the thought of death hadn't lifted from my mind I wanted to tell him how wrong he was.

I had no idea where Ilsa had gone. I was handicapped without the car and, after a short while, took a taxi to the Villa Miramar. The mail had been delivered since I went out and it included a letter from my agent to say that the serial rights of my last novel had been sold to a London newspaper. His note ended: *You lucky mortal. The weather's foul here and it's all I can do not to ask outright for an invitation. Or would I be de trop in that icing-sugar villa of yours? Your silence makes me wonder.* There was also a PS in his own hand: *How's the new book coming along?* His letters invariably resulted in elation or disappointment. It was the nature of our association. But now I felt neither pleasure nor gratitude. There was something unreal about the success and his last paragraph was as if he had wilfully pummelled a bruise. I threw the letter down. "Make-believe," Scheele had said, and make-believe was my trade; but I had lost touch with it.

Catalina emerged from the spare bedroom as I passed on my way to the hall.

141

"Buenos dias," I said. "I won't be eating in, either now or tonight."

She nodded. I would have gone by, but she began tenuously: "Señor—"

"Yes?"

Her date-brown eyes seemed sadly youthful in contrast to the walnut-wrinkled skin. "Captain Romero had me at his office yesterday. I haven't seen you since and I wanted to explain."

"I heard about it. It doesn't matter."

"I had to go. I dared not refuse."

"I understand. And I'm sorry you were sent for. But nothing's wrong."

"He asked many questions." Her concern was almost maternal. She would have been afraid of him: they all were. But she could be bold with me. "Impertinent questions."

"It was all a mistake," I said. "A misunderstanding"—and she clasped her hands with relief. By the time I had gone out to the car and filled the radiator she was singing with her usual contentment.

I drove back into the town. The sea was a shade less red but the beach was filthy and a few more swollen goats had come in, as stiff as bagpipes. At the Bar Sinbad I saw Joaquin moving purposefully between the outside tables, tray held high. He looked more at home there than on the plateau; innocent of secrets. It was strange to think that he knew less than I.

There was no sign of Ilsa and I decided against stopping to ask whether she had been in. I was coming to inflict pain and my mood wasn't pliable enough to indulge in deceiving him about his cousin. Later I must, always; but that I could learn to do.

I returned to the España and waited. Some men, they say, strew rags and dirt about the shrine at which they kneel, blaming the self-same gods for not making it possible for them to offer something finer. If, when Scheele had died, Ilsa's distress had not locked a door in my face I could have borne with it. I would never have been provoked into visiting Gondra or ransacked my brains for clues or questioned Joaquin or gone hopefully on the bus to meet Zavella. Only yesterday—was it yesterday? I had lost track—she had said that she couldn't bear to remain in ignorance of the reason for his death. How I was going to tell her I didn't know—or quite when. The only certainty was that she wouldn't believe me; would demand proof. Zavella was the immediate proof and I didn't want him on my conscience. But I needed to mention no names. "Someone I met" would do. The enormity of the disclosures would prolong her disbelief rather than provoke any desire to accuse. Repugnance and horror automatically generate incredulity and I, who had known Scheele for only a matter of days, still found myself giving way to it whenever I matched the man being buried in the morning against the slim, sandy-haired Condor Legion officer of Zavella's story. How much more, then, would she? There was an eight-year bond in his favour. But eventually—surely?—she would recoil from him; need me as never before. She couldn't blame me for telling her because she had wanted to know. And if there was spite in my motive—a sort of hatred, even—I was no more capable of seeing it than the blind can discern the shifting colours of the day. Desire, yes. Despair, yes. Love, yes. ... These three. Why else should I have armed myself as I had?

I took out the ring and examined it. A plump woman came to the bar and sat precariously on the stool next to mine and I covered the ring over quickly, like someone found out. I moved to a table; opened my fingers again. ES ... Schafer. Erich Schafer. ... What happened to you after Gondra? I thought. When did you become Scheele? There would be answers somewhere; all the proof in the world if need be.

People were continually coming in or leaving, but at last the sharp clack of Ilsa's heels sounded on the patterned tiles of the lobby and I put the ring away. Her step was instantly familiar—part of the trivia about her which my senses had amassed. She was wearing a dark grey costume and its severity emphasized her tanned pallor. As if I had every right to know, I said: "Where've you been?" One forgets that a lover has no rights; no responsibilities.

"To the shops."

"I've looked all over for you."

She hitched her skirt and sat down. "I went also to the agency about my flight."

"Oh?" There was a tightness in me; a sudden withering contraction. "When for?"

"Sunday," she said. "There is an Air France to Paris and I can make a connection there." The careful precision with which she always spoke, the slight lilt of her accent, conveyed an alarming determination.

"Must you?"

"Must I what?"

"Leave so soon?"

"Yes, Ty; I must." Then: "Can I have a cigarette, please?"

"But that's only two days from now." I was stunned.

"There is a lot to be seen to at home."

"I daresay. But—"

A waiter came, flicking a lighter. It seemed I wasn't even to be allowed to do that. The world was full of Boy Scouts. Woodenly, I ordered a dry sherry; watched the flame dance and the smoke curdle. Half a minute must have passed before either of us spoke again. A pendulum was swinging in my mind—"Tell her now. ... Don't tell her now." Under the concealed lighting her face was exquisitely beautiful. The lips whose watery taste I could still remember, the smooth forehead that the act of love had beaded with sweat, the small blue jugular vein on the side nearest me—I couldn't believe they weren't mine any more. Look at me, I thought. For God's sake look at me. ... The weapon was in my pocket. I had only to produce it to find a way through her indifference: then, like an armour-piercing shell, it would demolish her obsession. Grief and regret couldn't live with that I knew. The pendulum swung again and again: the half minute seemed endless. But what remained of my vanity wanted her without Scheele's aid: now that I was in her presence I would enlist him only if I must.

I said: "What about us, Ilsa?" I spoke quietly, in dread, leaning forward; but a burst of male laughter from the bar drowned my voice. To my dismay, she misheard. "Lunch? Yes. I was going to ask whether we could have it early. I want to go to the church afterwards. They're taking Erich there at two."

I sat back defeated, filled with venom.

"Will you come?" she asked.

"You won't want me."

"Ty." She said it gravely, dragged-out, as if she were reproving a child. Our eyes met at last and hers were tolerant with understanding. "I'd like you to."

I shrugged. "I'm no Catholic."

"Even so—"

"And I'm not sorry about anything either."

Now it was I who looked away; avoided her gaze. I could wound her worse than this. These were scratches.

"It's just as you wish," she said evenly.

"*You* are, though."

"I don't follow you."

"Sorry. ... You're sorry about us." My mind pleaded for a denial; unconsciously spelt out ESPAÑA on the ash-tray. Seconds passed.

"Oh, Ty."

I looked at her again. "That's not an answer."

She sighed. "Not now, Ty. Please."

"He's dead, Ilsa."

Her mouth went taut, as if I had struck her. She stubbed her cigarette in the big blue and white tray and stood up. "Forget I ever mentioned the church." She asked the waiter: "Is lunch possible?"

"Yes, señora."

I went with her, surrendering pride with every step. Heads swivelled to watch her pass; the buzz of general conversation faltered. But for me there was only bitterness in the rhythm of her stride. When we reached her table and were alone I said, with bad grace: "I'm sorry," but she didn't answer. For a long time we ate in brittle silence. The manager presented his compliments in person and we spoke to him almost as if we were strangers to one another. As he was about to bow himself away Ilsa asked if he would arrange for a taxi to be at the door at two o'clock.

"Of course, Señora Scheele."

I waited until he had gone. "That was quite unnecessary."

"It is too far to walk."

"You know very well I'll take you."

"I didn't and I don't."

"Well, I will."

"There's no point in your coming. You said so."

"I want to."

"Oh my God," she flared.

I had all but lost her. Without Scheele I could do nothing. Yet I still forbore to use him as my pimp. It may have been that I was too angry with myself; too wretched. Or that I sensed that to produce the ring in rage would have robbed my denunciation of its effectiveness. Whatever the reason I held my tongue and let what I knew continue to poison me.

Later: I had thought it yesterday and now I thought it again. I would tell her later, when she was calmer; when *I* was calmer. ...

We finished our coffee and left. A taxi was drawn up at the bottom of the flight of steps and I paid it off like a spoilt child; opened the door of my own car. Ilsa got in without a word and I drove her to her tryst with the ghost I was going to kill.

2

It was as dark as ever in the church. The wine-red sanctuary-lamp glowed through the permanent twilight; people moved like shadows, anonymous in their humility or on their conducted tour. On the huge suspended cross the nailed figure with the slumped head looked as if He slept. I let Ilsa precede me up the central aisle. Scheele was already there, the draped coffin to one side of the high altar, flanked with yellow tapers. She genuflected and such was my mood that her obeisance seemed almost as though it were directed towards him. I chose a seat two rows behind her; watched her kneel and bless herself. The flames of the thick candles guarding the coffin leaned as if stroked by an invisible hand, fluttered, then swelled and grew tall again. The old turkey-jowled priest came to her row, bending close, whispering secretly: his arrival was so prompt that it gave the impression he had been in wait for her. I should have feared him more, but I didn't believe that a few hours in a bed could result in an eternity of anguish. My hunger was for the body, and the soul was an intangible vapour; a memory in other minds.

The priest flapped away. I looked again at the coffin in its honoured position and wondered at which end Scheele's head was. "Real life and death—there's no substitute, Mister Tyler." He was my ally now, my last and only one—yet traitorously so, because Ilsa was thinking of him too. Her mind was dwelling on him in ignorance of the square at Gondra and the machine-guns hammering through the screams; or of the boy who hid in a cave and remembered the German officer who smoked a cigarette.

I rested my chin on clasped hands, though not to pray. Schafer; Scheele—whoever you were; whichever way they've put you round—it didn't end at Gondra, did it? Where did you go afterwards?—after you and the rest of your lot celebrated with that parade in Berlin? Was it Poland? Norway? France? Greece, perhaps? Russia? You went somewhere. Spain was merely the guinea-pig. You didn't hang your uniform on a peg in 1939—not with all that useful experience. Others like you went on to Warsaw, Lidice, the Ardennes. ... There were scores of places, each one of them a monstrous sin. Where did *you* go? And what happened that was sufficient to make you change your name? Wasn't Gondra enough for you?

A group of children scurried along the aisle; crowded a candle-lit saint. It didn't move as their rapt expressions seemed to expect.

Hier haben wir gewonnen. ... I thought: You didn't, Scheele—not personally; not in the end. You only imagined you had. If there's anything living left of you anywhere it must see that. By this evening Ilsa will have begun to believe me; started asking herself the same questions about you. And tomorrow she'll cancel her flight home.

The priest returned, surpliced; passed under an arch and went out of my view. I saw Ilsa bend her head lower. What use to Schafer were her prayers when she offered them up for Scheele? If I could have prayed, if I had felt that a plea would achieve something, I would have asked to be allowed to win my own victory, without Scheele's help. But God looked as if He were asleep, anyhow, and I was too twisted with selfishness to believe in any but my own powers. Lust suffereth little and is unkind. I could have reached forward and all but touched Ilsa's straight fair hair with my fingertips. The desire to do so was still active, but only Scheele could make contact possible.

She pushed herself off her knees. For a moment I assumed that she was leaving and half rose myself. But, instead, she moved crab-wise along the row of cane-seated chairs and disappeared in the direction the priest had taken. Turning, I saw her enter one of the confessionals in the side aisle. A curtain twitched: when she knelt down her shoes and slim calves protruded like a conjuror's assistant's. She couldn't have hurt or soured me more. I put my head in my hands. Is that why you asked me to come?—to humiliate me?—to let me witness it? I couldn't give her the benefit of the doubt that the priest may have urged it on her there and then. I knew of the formula: "Bless me, father, for I have sinned. ... Four or five times, father: on two separate occasions. ... No, never before. ..."

It was impossible to stay, listening to the imagined whispers. I got up and banged out of the church; found sunlight. On the worn steps I stood and stared at the flower-sellers that Christ would have ordered away; at the sprinklers vainly at work among the patterns of diseased grass. The whispered repudiation was lodged in my ears and I entered an intensity of despair such as I had never known. The thought formed like an angry fist: All right, then. You've asked for it now.

Ilsa was inside a long time. I waited in the car. Even hatred has periods of calm—and what was this but hatred? I smoked through two cigarettes; willed her to come before reason applied a blunting edge. Jealousy builds the narrowest of bridges between enmity and desire; sometimes fuses the two.

At last she came—shriven, presumably; pure again, washed clean of me. I said coldly: "You needn't have been so obvious about it."

"I'm sorry. But it was not intentional."

"Rubbish." I crashed a gear.

"That's true."

"I'm surprised you should even risk re-contamination."

The word defeated her but I had said enough. "Don't make it worse for me, Ty."

"For you!"

"Yes, for me."

A wobbling Vespa slowed us down. "You loved me once," I said. "Does a set of rules kill all that? They didn't mean much to you while he was alive."

Her voice was low; the restraint fresh from absolution. "Try not to hate me, please."

"I don't understand you. And I haven't got time to be delicate—not if you're walking out on me on Sunday."

"I must do that."

"I don't see why."

The España was in view and I swung the car across the

road through a gap in the traffic. The manoeuvre checked her reply. We were gritting into the kerb before she said: "I've already told you why."

"You're free now—rules or no rules. I repeat: I don't understand. What about you and me?"

"It wouldn't work." She shook her head.

"You've hardly tried."

"I could never forget that I was with you when Erich died. Never."

"He's best forgotten."

She wheeled on me, restraint ebbing fast. "You mustn't say a thing like that."

"I'll say it again. He's best forgotten. You don't know what sort of person—"

She was out of the car before I had finished. I caught her up near the top of the steps; gripped her by the arm. She wrenched it away but I regained it. "D'you think I enjoy doing this?"

"Go away."

"No. You come with me."

The reception-desk staff eyed me curiously as I led Ilsa into the American Bar. She didn't want to sit down but I insisted, saying: "I've got something here you ought to see."

"What d'you mean?"

"Your property."

I took out the ring and handed it to her. Surprise softened her expression a little. "But this is Erich's."

"Of course."

"Where on earth did you find it?"

"I didn't. It was given me."

A waiter approached. "Later," I said.

"*Given* to you?"

I nodded, watching her earnestly. Now it was coming.

"Who by?"

"I don't know who he was."

She fingered the ring; brushed the onyx with a thumb. "It was one of the things stolen from our room."

"I know." Were we so estranged?

"When did you get it?"

I should have been less honest. "I heard about it the other day. I actually got my hands on it this morning."

"And you didn't tell me?"

"I have now."

"Do you mean you've known of it all this time and never said a word? That's unfair and unkind."

"I was anxious not to disappoint you." Her gaze accused, hardening my heart. I said bluntly: "Are those Erich's initials?"

She looked from me to the ring; from the ring back to me. "Of course they are."

"Erich Scheele?"

She frowned, mystified. "What are you talking about? It's his ring."

Someone at my elbow said: "Señor Tyler?" I thought it was the waiter again; turned irritably to find a uniformed message-boy, ridiculous in a pill-box hat.

"What is it?"

"Telephone, señor."

"You must be mistaken. I'm not a guest here."

"For Señor Tyler." He blinked and spoke like a parrot.

"Who's asking for me?"

"I don't know, señor."

His timing was a conspiracy. I glanced at Ilsa. The denunciation was on the tip of my tongue—"It may have been his ring but that wasn't his name. He fooled you. His name was Schafer and twenty years ago he destroyed Gondra and everyone in it. Murdered them. That's why he's best forgotten." It would have been a dramatic exit-line; something to return to and bludgeon home. But I faltered and said: "Excuse me, will you."

I followed the boy into the lobby; was shown the booth. The door padded, sealing me in.

"Yes?" The mouthpiece was damp with another's condensed breath. "Tyler here."

"This is Captain Romero."

"Oh?"

Wherever he was he cleared his throat. "I have a favour to ask."

"You've come to the wrong person."

"I'm not asking it for myself."

"Don't tell me you have friends."

"The favour is asked by a friend of yours, señor. At least, he claims that distinction."

"Who?"

Romero let it drop like a stone. "Luis Zavella."

There was absolute quiet in the booth. A rustle of paper reached me along the line. "Zavella?"

"Yes. He wants to speak to you."

It could have been a trick. "Put him on then. I'm listening."

"That is hardly possible. But I know where he is; where you can reach him."

My heart was sinking. I stalled: "So?"

"We've got him bottled up in The White Caves."

Silence again as my thoughts whirled. "And he wants to speak to me?"

"So he says."

The verb implied close contact between them. "For what reason?"

"I am as curious as you, señor. All I can tell you is that he will be dead in half an hour if you don't come."

"And if I do?"

He was cryptic. "Something might be arranged."

"It'll take me the best part of half an hour to get there."

"As long as I know you're coming I will wait."

"I'm coming," I said. "Now."

I took a deep breath and backed grimly out of the booth. Ilsa was still fondling the ring when I reached the table. "I'm sorry but I've been called away. It's urgent. I'll explain later."

What I did and where I went were of no interest to her any more. Her only question was: "Why did you ask if these were Erich's initials?"

152

For a long moment I held her puzzled gaze. Now—of all people—it was Zavella who conspired against her knowing: the irony bit deep. But it would have been a crime to squander even a few minutes of his half hour. Why he wanted me I couldn't imagine, unless it were to blame me for having put Romero on his track. Uncertainty elbowed my vendetta with Scheele aside. I stared hard at Ilsa, mentally protesting my innocence.

"We'll talk when I get back."

Seconds afterwards I was going down the hotel steps, two at a time. And of the faces which haunted me on the drive—hers, Zavella's, Scheele's, Romero's, Joaquin's—it was that of the rabbit on the rack of the morning bus which overprinted them all.

CHAPTER NINE

1

THE bus had taken twenty minutes to reach the bridge which spanned the gorge: I did it in twelve, laying a spreading trail of dust over wayside crops, exploding birds out of trees. The road was fairly clear and only once—because of a shepherdless flock of sheep—was I reduced to a crawl. The White Caves were a kilometre or so beyond the bridge but I reckoned that Romero would hear me coming before I even crossed it. The snort-snort of my horn trumpeted off the hills at every snickering corner.

The first of his guards was positioned on the far side of the gorge. Some kind of road-control was apparently in operation because the man made a half-hearted attempt to stop me, jumping clear when he thought better of it. Some distance further on a notice-board read:

THE WHITE CAVES

UNIQUE AND ORIGINAL FORMATIONS

OWN ELECTRICOL PLANT

I had been there before, like any tourist, and didn't need the help of the arrowed direction sign when the road presently split left and right:

400 METRES

THE WHITE CAVES

OPEN EVERY DAY FROM 10 TO 20 HRS

I turned beneath a bulging, lichen-grey cliff. Just past the

154

fork there were two guards standing in the middle of the camber; beyond them, a Perspex-topped coach. Freshly tanned faces peered through its windows as I slowed. There wasn't enough room to force past at speed. An exasperated young woman was protesting to the guards: "This is a scandal. My organization has a contract with the Caves— every Monday, Wednesday and Friday. What right have you to forbid us to go any further?"

They ignored her; moved over to me. "Señor Tyler?" one asked.

I nodded.

"Captain Romero is at the hut."

I thought I knew where he meant; dropped into gear. Drawing away, I heard the woman complain volubly: "Why should *he* be allowed to go up? I've got thirty-four people here..."

The road curled under the craggy wall of rock: at regular intervals white posts marked the brink of the gorge. A tight bend was followed by another. Then the road straightened and pointed towards the entrance of the caves, widening as it did so, to form an oval-shaped area large enough to accommodate a sanded car park, a café and several souvenir stalls. Normally crowded, the car park was empty except for a solitary Seat saloon and about a dozen red and black motorcycles. Every waiter, stall-attendant and guide had disappeared. A score of guards made a rough semi-circle near the dark mouth of the caves, their rifles unslung and variously at the ready. The sight of them chilled whatever hopes I had entertained for Zavella. Was I responsible? The persistent doubt flowed through every bleak and poisoned part of me. I braked near the big Seat and got out; walked over to the wooden ticket-office. There was a side door which opened into a small room lined with shelves stacked with rolls of coloured tickets. Romero was sitting on a table talking into the telephone. He didn't notice me immediately and swung an immaculate leg, delighted with himself.

"... that's correct. Oh no—quite impossible. ... Yes. ... Very good, I'll report back within the hour. ... What was that?" He listened, then nodded, chuckling. "Thank you very much."

He rang off; smoothed his tunic. Only then did he see me. "You were quick." His moustache accentuated his slightly embarrassed smirk.

"I know the road."

He gave no hint that he was aware of it. With an attempt at blandness, he said: "There is an English proverb, I believe: 'A friend in need is a friend indeed'."

"I didn't come to hear you air your knowledge."

"But you came—and fast."

"I was asked for."

He touched his moustache gingerly, as if it pained him. "You told me the other day that you had never heard of Luis Zavella."

"Maybe I did."

"Yet you were the one person he mentioned when I spoke to him. Would you care to explain?"

"Not to you."

He warded off my contempt with one of his shrugs.

I said: "What d'you mean—'spoke to him'? Isn't he inside the caves?"

"There's a speaking-tube near the turnstiles. The guides use it to make sure that parties of tourists don't tread on each other's heels. It's a control. When a guide with one group gets to a certain point he reports to the turnstiles; then the next one starts off."

A beetle laboured across the floor, advertising life. Some men can be appealed to; bribed. But not Romero.

"When I was in the España you said something might be arranged."

He nodded. "I wondered if you could persuade Zavella to give himself up."

"That won't be why he's asked for me."

"I want you to try."

"Say he won't?"

"Then we will go in. But it would be better if there were no shooting."

Through the wire mesh of the ticket aperture I could see the semi-circle of guards waiting in the hot afternoon sun. Misgivings dragged at my heart.

Romero went on: "Zavella has all the advantages in there. Otherwise I wouldn't have called you. To catch a fox one must become a fox—that is a proverb in *my* country."

The feeling of guilt boiled over. "How did you know where he was?"

"A corporal of mine saw him enter."

"Just that?"

"Just that. The corporal was off-duty, with some friends from Madrid." Romero must have noticed my relief. "Was it troubling you, Señor Tyler?"

I looked at him hard. "Yes, it was." Then I said: "What will happen to him if he decides to come out?"

"He'll be tried and sentenced." He paused; crunched the beetle with a gleaming shoe. "Either way he will die."

"For what reason?"

"For murder."

He knew, then. "Whose?"

"Señor Scheele's." He narrowed his eyes a little. "I expected you would show more surprise. It must be a weight off your mind."

"Perhaps I will if you can prove it."

"We have the gun. It was brought in yesterday from Gondra. It is one of two rifles which he stole from the guard-house by the Lareo Dam last year."

"And that's proof?"

"For me, yes. When it's someone like Zavella, yes."

Why I persisted I don't know. Zavella was doomed. Perhaps it was because I felt that the seeds which men like Scheele had planted continued to bear fruit in others like Romero: the pitiless strain still flourished given the conditions. Whatever the reason, I said passionately: "What do you know of Zavella?"

"Enough to finish him. No more is necessary."

I made for the door like someone in need of air. Romero followed; fell into step with me. Success had thickened his skin. The prospect of promotion sounded in the gritty strike of his heels. The line of guards stirred expectantly as we passed through and approached the turnstiles: beyond them the rock-face ahead of us tunnelled sharply in towards the gaping entrance of the caves. The turnstiles clicked round under the pressure of our hips. A sergeant occupied a recess in the left-hand wall near the plugged end of the speaking-tube. It was tacked along the rock like a cable, shoulder-high. Nearby was a lidded power-switch and—on the ground —four wooden boxes.

Romero tapped a foot against one of these. "Tear gas," he explained. "If the worst comes to the worst we must take every precaution. Have you explored the caves?"

"I've been round."

"Then you will appreciate my responsibility. They're unique. One centimetre of stalactite takes a hundred years to form." He ordered the sergeant to switch on the lights: the tunnel was suddenly bright and inviting, white-washed as far as the eye could see. "Do what you can to make him realize how hopeless it is."

The sergeant eased out of the recess. Romero un-plugged the speaking-tube and blew into it, his sallow cheeks ballooning. He blew twice, waited a moment, then spoke. "Zavella?" It seemed impossible that his voice was carrying beyond the visible limits of the tunnel. "Zavella?" He put an ear to the tube, neat eyebrows pinched together as he concentrated. Presently, he was acknowledged. I heard nothing, but he suddenly nodded and transferred his mouth to the cup-like aperture. "I'm sending your friend in now." A pause. "D'you hear me, Zavella? Your friend, Señor Tyler, is coming in now."

Apparently satisfied, he plugged the tube-end; addressed me. "I will be here should you wish to speak about anything."

"It's unlikely."

"You never know. But remember—if he has some idea of using you to his advantage—as a hostage, say—it will not dissuade me from taking the necessary measures."

"I can look after myself."

"So long as you appreciate the position. ... Have you a watch?"

"Yes."

"It's just coming up to ten-past four. I'll give you until half-past."

"I'm not being 'given' anything," I said. "Let's get that straight here and now. I'll come out when I choose—and not before."

It is possible that if his sergeant had not been present Romero might have taken it more coolly. As it was he began to bluster: the smooth veneer was surprisingly thin. "You seem to forget who you're talking to. When I say I'll give you until half-past—"

"I forget nothing where you're concerned. Nothing, d'you understand? I'm here because of Zavella; not on behalf of you or a caveful of stalactites. There'll always be another million years."

I left him standing; felt his anger boring into my back as I made for the entrance. I was sweating, ice and fire, though not because of the heat. In four languages a notice by the tunnel's mouth forbade smoking. The English version was written: NO SMOKING ALOUD. A worn cement floor threw the sound of my step on to rough-hewn walls and ceiling, deadening it, making it at once flat yet metallic. Names were occasionally scribbled on the walls; initials, dates. Two I remember to this day—HARRY MILNE 1957 ... BILL AND RENE, DURHAM, U.S.A. ...

The air was warm and damp; smelt vaguely urinal. Like flint arrowheads, moths basked in the light around each naked bulb. The tunnel sloped gently downwards. After about forty yards it suddenly opened out into the first of the caverns. One moment I was in a functional whitewashed pipe; the next in a world of utter fantasy. Hidden illuminations silhouetted a multitude of grotesque and astonishing forms. Months before, the guide had paused and said mechanically: "The Entrance Hall, ladies and gentlemen, discovered by accident in 1910. The dominant colour is the result of a concentration of calcium carbonate. The stalactite formations here are characteristic of the entire caves. ..." But now I walked straight through, following the railed, undulating path, moving cautiously because of the gloom. The speaking-tube was somewhere, but I couldn't see it. Where the cavern narrowed I stopped under a draped curtain of transparent stone.

"Zavella?"

A swift echo: then silence, eerie and total. I moved on through a glistening archway and found myself in the second cave, larger and more lofty than the first. The concealed lighting was bluish-white. Here were The Candle Factory and The Enchanted Garden, The Ruined Castle and The Snowy Mountain. It was a place for innocent wonder, not for dying in. I was coming like a priest, alone and confidential, yet bringing nothing except an awful sense of inadequacy. Why had he asked for me? I was powerless to help: he must have known that. Why then? For what?

"Zavella?" I called softly.

"A-a-a-ah." The echo was followed by a single plop of dripping water, that was all. I had a fleeting, almost deranged belief that I was talking to myself; was completely alone. A freakish stalagmite—Saint Christopher, according to the guide—stood in a natural alcove, cunningly lit from behind. I moved on again, reassured by the existence of the railing; sometimes, when the path dipped, resting a hand on a damp upright. Banded, fluted, tapering, goitred—the spindly pinnacles grew everywhere, reaching up in vertical monotony towards the spiked, petrified roof, sometimes achieving union. The pumice-like stone was as warm and smooth as skin. Each few yards transformed the dioramic vistas; opened up others. I passed into The Hall of Flags. There was still no answer when I called but I was beginning to sense that Zavella wasn't far away. The lights flickered alarmingly, held on, brightened. I suppose I had been inside for no more than a couple of minutes yet already it seemed many times as long.

"It's me ... Tyler."

The flat echoes were all squeezed tight together, like a flutter of wings. Zavella was watching me, I knew; making sure, straining his eyes. The feeling of being observed was physical; unnerving. I remained still, the quiet like wadding in my ears. Then I heard him cough, and though I had been waiting for some clue to his whereabouts the hollow bark raised the short hairs on my neck.

"Zavella?" I looked about me, peering left and right, tense. "Where are you?"

And at last he said:

"I'm here, Señor Tyler."

Even then I couldn't distinguish him: he had to move first. To my left was a grotto which held The Chessmen—a packed formation of stalagmites adequately enough shaped and grouped to justify the name. Zavella's silhouette was partly merged into that of an approximation to a horse-headed Knight. The grotto was slightly above the level of the path and his thin, scarecrow body looked somehow larger than life. A cold shiver brushed my nerves before recognition slackened them off. I started towards him, but he checked me; slithered down, clutching his rifle.

I said: "I'd never have seen you."

"Good." He was thinking ahead. Close though we were the light wasn't sufficiently strong for me to notice the play of his features, but his handshake conveyed emotion to an extraordinary degree. "Thank you for coming."

"What brought you in here?—of all places?" It was a lament.

"It's an old route of mine. A short cut."

"*This* is?"

"I've a friend on the gates."

"But it's such an obvious trap."

"Not normally. There's another way out—a fissure which leads far back to the top of the cliff. I've used it for years.

I doubt if more than half-a-dozen people knew of it. But today, when I needed it most, it failed me. The rains have blocked it up."

"Tell me what happened."

"Someone recognized me—a guard. I was through the turnstiles when the shouting started, but I wasn't much concerned. A group of people had just finished going round and I had the place to myself. I didn't even run after I was past here—I was that confident. Then I discovered the fissure was blocked. They'd put the lights out by that time."

"And then?"

"I used up every match I had finding my way back to the tube."

"Where's that?"

'Behind you." He pointed. "I couldn't hope to get as far as the tunnel in the dark. The railing isn't continuous and I'd have lost myself. It would have been too late, anyhow: I knew that. I waited here for a while—a long while. Ayee, it seemed like days. Eventually, I blew into the tube and spoke to someone who fetched Romero."

He coughed: once I had imagined it would be the cough that would destroy him.

"They've got your gun," I said. "The one you threw away at Gondra."

He nodded, face profiled. "Romero told me. ... You're talking to a dead man, señor."

"If you stay here, yes."

"Here—outside; it'll make no difference."

"If they heard your story they'd take a less serious view."

He scoffed quietly. "'They'!"

"I'm sure of it."

"'They' are Romero and others like him, with or without uniform."

"They're not all the same. Your defence at a trial would give you the opportunity—"

"You're speaking about some other country, Señor Tyler. I'd be found in one of Romero's cells with my throat cut before there was any trial. They don't want the past raked over."

Thinking he might have asked me to enlist my advocacy, I said: "I'll tell them."

"They wouldn't listen."

"I'd make them."

"No. Thank you, but no." He shook his head. Clearly he had come to a decision with himself during his wait in the darkness. "I prefer The White Caves." All the bravado had gone. His voice trembled as he controlled his fear. "At least I've got this." The butt of the rifle grated on the path: I presume he had carried it past the turnstiles down a trousers' leg, though at the time I accepted his having it without question.

"You won't have a chance."

"More than they had at Gondra."

I saw his Adam's-apple bounce. A drop of water fell and the tiny splash sounded like a living thing. Above our heads were The Flags of Many Nations. "Notice the colours," the guide had said, "and the way each hanging sheet of stone is folded as if a breeze is blowing." But there was no breeze and never would be. The grave would be like this, for ever and ever.

Zavella said: "I first came in here when I was a boy—with my father. I remember him telling me that I'd never see any change even if I came back in a thousand years. ... Ayee." The sigh was like a prayer. "How right he was. It seems like that."

The lights flickered again. He took a cigarette from me; eagerly lowered his lean face towards the match as if he thirsted. The flame bobbed as he drew and I had a brief glimpse of his suffering. I could hardly grasp that it was nearly over. As if to try and shake my disbelief I handed him the packet and the box, but even his fumbling acceptance of them seemed part of the unreality.

Yet I said: "Won't you change your mind?"

"No." His profile was dark again, etched against the soft, orange illumination of The Chessmen.

"Then why did you send for me?"

He coughed. "I wanted to ask you about the señora."

163

"What about her?"

"Does she know?"

"About you?"

"About Schafer."

"Not yet."

The glow of his cigarette brightened; dimmed. "Don't tell her," he said.

"I must."

"No." The echo fluttered. "There's no need."

I said uneasily: "He was her husband."

"But she had finished with him. It was over."

I was silent, nails digging into my palms. The sense of unreality reached out to include Ilsa. Was she still in the American Bar?—still nursing the ring?

Zavella said: "That is so, isn't it?"

Vanity made a final stand. "Yes."

"Never tell her then. That's all I ask."

Water dripped somewhere. I shut my eyes. Don't extract a promise from me. I'll break it as soon as I'm clear of here. Don't make me despise myself more than I do already.

"I was a long time alone in the dark," Zavella continued. "I thought about this more than anything else. It's the only reason I asked Romero to get in touch with you."

"The truth will come out." My voice was low. "You had no other motive."

"Robbery."

"But Scheele wasn't robbed."

"The dam-burst prevented it." He paused. "Romero's satisfied with that. Why tell her something different if you love her?"

You're dead, I thought. I can't pretend that I'm dead, too.

Zavella said: "Hatred is a disease. Why pass it on to her? It could eat her away from the inside just as it's eaten me away. I've had it for twenty years. It disfigures you; cripples you. And in the end it destroys you." The cough shook him gently. "I wish it on nobody."

I shook my head in silent protest.

164

"She would never forgive you."

The whistle in the end of the tube sounded impatiently. I wrenched out the plug and let it dangle from its chain. A faint bleat came from the aperture.

"She would never forgive you," Zavella repeated.

I stared at him as if he had betrayed me.

"Have you given her the ring?"

"Yes." Then I said hopelessly: "What about *my* hatred? Where's the cure for that?"

Inevitably, he misunderstood. "Why should you hate Schafer? He's neither destroyed nor deceived you. You've won, in fact. Hang on to your victory, Señor Tyler."

The aperture bleated a second time, nudging shame into me. Romero wouldn't delay much longer. Zavella must have been wanting me to say: "If that's your wish I'll honour it." But I was too split in myself to be able to speak.

"Don't tell Joaquin either," he said.

I nodded.

"It would be a burden for him. He could never keep it to himself. He'd clash with Romero and bring much trouble on his head. Let him know you saw me, though."

"Of course."

He dropped his cigarette and the glow hissed on the damp stone. "Good-bye, then." He was abrupt.

I urged desperately: "Walk out with me and stand trial."

Zavella shook his head. He shifted the gun beyond my reach, almost as if he suspected me of selfish intentions.

With a gesture of impotent helplessness, I argued: "They've got tear gas."

"I'll welcome it. It is a lifetime since I cried." He drew himself up, afraid, yet with dignity. As he faced me the light from The Chessmen touched his beard-stubble; softened one sunken cheek. "Good-bye, Señor Tyler."

I could hardly trust myself to look at him. "Good-bye."

"Many years," he wished me and the poignancy of the phrase forced the words emotionally off my tongue: "I won't forget what you've said."

165

"I know you won't."

I began to grope along the railing. What I was doing didn't seem possible. I felt sick. I heard Zavella moving behind me, presumably coming to select a vantage-point nearer the tunnel, but I didn't look back. The Hall of Flags ended and I passed between the forest of petrified stems of The Enchanted Garden, blind to it, an agony of distress beating a tattoo against my senses. By the time the light of the terrace showed up I could hear Zavella no longer. I saw the speaking-tube snake in from the walls of The Entrance Hall and the path led me back to where time existed; where there was a future and no peace.

The sun poured into my eyes. There seemed to be even more guards than when I went in. I bawled at them, beside myself: "There's only one man in there! ... *One man!*" Romero was by the speaking-tube. He came towards me as I walked, closing in from the side with the stiff-legged suspicion of a dog approaching another.

"Is he coming out?"

"No."

A sluggish breeze twirled some torn-up tickets across the sanded clearing. I pushed through the turnstiles, Romero lengthening his stride in an effort to draw level.

"What did he want you for?"

I didn't answer.

"What did he want you for?"

I grimaced against the light. A guard shifted out of my way. Romero was almost at my shoulder.

"Señor Tyler!" He tried to grasp my arm but I shook him off, making for the car. "Why did he want to talk to you?"

I opened the car door and got in; slammed it after me. The hood was down. I touched the starter and the engine fired.

Romero raged: "I demand an answer, Señor Tyler. What did Zavella want?"

"Go in and ask him," I said in a voice that didn't sound like my own. "He's waiting for you."

2

I stopped at a flaking wayside bar about a mile short of the town and drank three or four quick brandies, standing at the counter. A caged canary above the radio rocked on a metal swing and the woman who served me tried to tempt it with a piece of stale black sausage.

"How much?"

"Twelve pesetas."

A hysterical impulse made me say: "I want the bird as well."

She laughed, gap-toothed. "Paco is not for sale, señor. I'm sorry." Nevertheless she asked: "What would you do with it?"

"Set it free."

"But it would die." She was indignant and muttered resentfully. "What a thing to suggest! It would be killed."

I drove off, the nauseous feeling gaining ground. I promised him nothing, I thought. Nothing. I just said I wouldn't forget. That's not a promise. ...

It had gone five: they'd be inside the caves. Hurry it up, for God's sake. Finish with it. ... My mind's eye kept seeing Zavella, not the dark silhouette by The Chessmen but as he was in the Villa Miramar when I confronted him with the ridiculous cigarette-lighter and he said: "Time is an ambush, señor." You're right, poor bastard, I thought. It was for Scheele and it's proved so for you. ...

I passed the España. I couldn't force myself to go in and rejoin Ilsa: not so soon. I went on as far as the Bar Sinbad and parked under the plane trees, crossed the road and sat at one of Joaquin's tables. But another waiter tended me; balding, stooped.

"Where's Joaquin?"

"Off duty, señor. Since lunchtime."

I glanced across the square at the Civil Guard building. So he'd heard; someone had slipped him the news. I was relieved it wouldn't have to be me: the last hour had made me a coward.

167

"Family trouble, I believe," the waiter remarked. "What can I get you?"

"Bring some Fundador."

Some boys played with a ball by the central fountain and their shrill happiness insulted everything that haunted me. I told myself: Even if I *did* make him a promise I'm not bound by it. He didn't know what he was asking.

The waiter came with a new bottle; peeled the lead foil and drew the cork. "Leave it," I said. He wasn't used to me and I all but had to take it from him.

Zavella would be dead by now. ... I drank, watching the light fade, unmindful of time. I had been spared Joaquin. I would see his long, pained features soon enough—tomorrow, the day after: I could suffer with him then and perpetuate the lies. A week hence, even. But tomorrow and the day after were all that remained where Ilsa was concerned. Yet I continued to sit and drink; made no effort to return to the España. "She would never forgive you." Was that why? I put my hands over my ears, as if to stop the flow of memory. I was coward enough without Zavella's logic.

Dusk came, thickening fast. Lights were switched on around the square and in the Civil Guard headquarters; above the crowded tables. I thought I saw Romero's car slide in but it had grown too dark for me to be sure. The bottle was a third empty. I was already unforgiven. Only a few hours ago she had said: "I could never forget that I was with you when Erich died." Never forgive, never forget. ... The weapon I had so assiduously forged was ready too late. "Hang on to your victory, Señor Tyler." What victory? If I honoured any promise it would be because of defeat. ...

The brandy burned deeper, deadening all but pain. Around me were the ebb and flow of laughter, music, voices. Someone came and sat opposite me; a man, fifty-ish, with a thirty-six hour tan. I didn't reply when he first spoke. Later, he inquired: "Are you feeling all right?" I raised my head. There were two of him, both as soft-edged as a dream. "All right?" he asked and I nodded, gripping my glass.

"You're British, aren't you?"

"How did you guess? I usually insist on a flag on the table."

My tongue apparently couldn't cope with acid because he gave a smug smile, approving his discernment. "I can generally tell. Sort of sixth sense—you know? My missus hasn't got it at all. Yesterday, for instance, she made a most frightful bloomer. ..."

I thought: Ilsa. Oh God. Ilsa.

Presently I heard: "I say—you ought to go easy with that stuff, you know." His two images came momentarily together: buck teeth, wiry hair, pointed chin. "The vino's so damned cheap in these parts that one forgets one's not used to it. A fellow-director of mine—"

"I'm drinking for a friend." I wasn't able to hold the focus.

"But—"

He stopped short. I stared blearly into the square, alone with my wretched permutations of Ilsa and Scheele, Zavella and Romero and Joaquin, corrupted with the conviction that I had been cheated out of what was mine. Slowly, glass by glass, I was learning that there are other ways of dying.

Dimly, I realized the man was warming to a new topic. "My missus and I come to Spain every year. It's different, you know: I always say Africa begins at the Pyrenees. And we try and get acquainted with the people—the real peasants. No organized tours for us, thank *you*. They're fifty years behind the times here, of course, but they've got something we lack at home. The old virtues—honour, decency, courage, patience, manners. ... I told my missus only today that it's a result of a combination of the acceptance of the Catholic and the fatalism of the Moor. To suffer is to live, after all. ... I'll put up with the plumbing and the way they knock their animals around just to—"

My chair screeched as I pushed it back and got up. A glass went over. I lurched away from him. The man complained loudly: "You're a rude sod, I must say!" I blundered through the purple streets and found refuge in another bar, strewn with sawdust and with brass spittoons beside every marble-topped table. It would have been easier to cry but, like Zavella, I seemed to have lost the ability. A flamenco singer chanted nasally, simulating emotion, yet the cheap words had a terrible potency:

> *The roses we plucked*
> *Are all thrown away,*
> *But sharp thorns*
> *Are still in my flesh. ...*

I'll never know how long I stayed or where else I went. Afterwards, in the Street of Jesus and Mary, a girl with a crimson mouth whispered from a shadowy doorway, but one can lust and still be faithful and I wanted nobody but Ilsa.

A taxi eventually took me home. At least, that's where I found myself next morning, with hope drained out of me and the taste of death in my mouth.

CHAPTER TEN

1

I WAS late at the church: Scheele's Requiem Mass was already in progress when. I tiptoed to a seat. Ilsa I saw at once. She was alone in the front row of chairs, not more than three yards from where the black-draped coffin rested on its catafalque at the foot of the sanctuary steps. The old priest was at the altar, gabbling his way through the Mass as if it were some private rite of no concern to the hunched congregation. The number of people present surprised me. Some, no doubt, were routine worshippers, accustomed to be there at eleven o'clock. But others had come for a specific reason. Romero was one of these; the manager of the España another. I noticed the Mayor and his wife, the proprietor of the Bar Sinbad and an official from the Tourist Office. I asked myself leadenly if they had never winced and bristled at Scheele's arrogance; never seen the contempt in which he had held them all? Was I the only one who hated him? And, if that were so, would I have been as blind as the rest of them if he had had no wife and I had never learned his secret? One key had opened many doors, though never the one I wished to enter.

I watched Ilsa from my place at the back. As recently as yesterday I would have been jealous of her proximity to the coffin, but I was too weary to be irrational any more. The priest went about his business—murmuring, gesticulating, genuflecting—offering up the unfathomable mystery on behalf of Scheele. Yes, I suppose I should have feared him more, but I couldn't grapple with what I didn't understand. It was strange to think that he would have been my implacable

171

enemy if Scheele had lived—he and half a million like him. But Ilsa was free now. The only restraint to which she was subjected came from within herself—and Scheele had planted it there as surely as he had once used Spain as a seed-bed for brutality and wickedness. And for both these things I knew that I would go on loathing him until the end of my days.

I had come a long way since Zavella died. But one can sever a limb and still feel the pain in it; cut out one's tongue and still have to curb the urge to speak. When Ilsa went to the altar-rails and took the bloodless bread I had enough bitterness left to think: What about me? What about Zavella? Or don't the losers count?

The Mass ended. Half a dozen stocky men came forward and lifted the coffin on to their shoulders with professional reverence. This time I could see which end of the box was which. They brought Scheele up the aisle head first and I wondered briefy as he passed whether his facial muscles remained taut with terror.

There were three cars at the door besides the hearse. The mourners sorted themselves from the rest of the congregation. I rode in the first car with Ilsa and a man I had seen in the church but couldn't place. Ilsa introduced us perfunctorily: he was from the German Consulate in Barcelona. We acknowledged one another gravely. Ilsa was dressed in the same dark costume she had worn the previous afternoon, in addition to which her head was covered with a black veil. Except for introducing me to the German she did not speak. She had cried recently; her eyes were puffy. The brandy had left a pump hammering in my head and I would have preferred not to have had to sit on the tip-down seat facing her. It would have been more comfortable beside her, but the German had got there first.

I tried to look everywhere but at her. Occasionally people blessed themselves as we passed them in the streets. There seemed no end to those who would honour Scheele. Alive, I could have exposed him and watched him destroy his place in Ilsa's heart. But now he was sacrosanct. He'd won here after all—each time he'd come: and only I knew it.

It was a ten-minute ride to the cemetery. I had never been there before and not knowing how far we were going somehow made the journey seem longer. Once we were clear of Bandaques the road was unsurfaced and the hearse raised a pall of dust for us to grind through. The windows grew dirty and the German sweated a great deal. We stopped once and I presumed we had arrived, but some of the wreaths had apparently fallen from the hearse and we had to wait until the attendants collected them. The three of us swayed in unison as the car rocked over the inevitable potholes, separately concerned with grief and defeat and—I imagine— the bore of duty. I thought it likely that Romero had already told Ilsa about Zavella. He would have been full of himself last evening; a knight in shining armour. Murdered for gain. ... The knowledge could account for the air of injustice moulded so clearly into her outward and visible distress, and for that reason alone I feared catching her eye. It takes courage to surrender the truth without hope of reward.

When we next stopped it was at the cemetery—a huge walled rectangle of weather-beaten sandstone on a desolate slope above the town. A brown, blind woman squatted beside the open gates on a rush-plaited chair surrounded by a number of yellow clay pitchers. I suppose she was there to sell water, but—those on the hearse apart—the only flowers I could see were artificial; inside the walls the tombs and rusting crosses under the dark cypresses standing like fixed explosions against the noonday sky were decorated with nothing else.

We filed in behind the coffin—nine of us, together with the priest and a boy assistant. The boy, at least, made no bones about his indifference. But the Mayor and his wife and the rest put on the required faces as they gathered round the boarded pit. Romero's, in particular, was detestable. For the first time in days I looked at Ilsa with something like charity. Across the narrow width of the grave my mind asked

173

her indignantly: Why are they here? Who are they? You're the only one who's suffering. I've come because of you, not because of Scheele-cum-Schafer. But at least I know who he was—and you think you know. ...

I studied some of the tombstones nearest me. A worn plaque read: RUBIO SALINAS; GONDRA, 12.4.1938. YOUR MOTHER WILL NOT FORGET YOU. ... FRANCISCO DIAZ; GONDRA, 12.4.1938. ... ESPERANZA CABRER; GONDRA, 12.4.1938. HONOURED FOR EVER. ... The false roses and mimosa, brittle and bleached with age, belied the vain promises. The priest had begun to scatter earth on to the lowered coffin: it landed with a hollow sound, as if the varnished box were empty. The wreaths lying on the heaps of stony red soil were fresh and indecently beautiful—lilies and carnations and iris predominated. Only a couple of cards were readable from where I stood. One merely said: FROM ILSA. She had printed it, as a child might. The other was from Romero: WITH DEEP AND LASTING REGRET. The flourish of his signature was as preposterous as the wording.

The priest closed his missal: it was all over. Dust to dust. ... Ilsa scooped earth into the pit and the others followed suit. I turned away and walked slowly back to the gate. A corroded, three-flapped piece of metal on which a likeness to the Virgin was embossed hung loosely from a nail above a tomb set in the wall. The plaque bore the names of Zavella's father and mother—TOMEO CANALS and MARIA ZAVELLA DE CANALS. There was no pious declaration cut into the stone; merely the place and the date—GONDRA, 12.4.1938.

The irony was complete. And I thought: Good-bye, Schafer. They've all been waiting for you.

We climbed back into the cars after Ilsa had shaken hands with everyone except the German consular official and me. I sat beside her on the return run, tongue-tied, my head still hammering. The German smoked. Like me, he couldn't find anything to say but the regulation mourning-look was beginning to crack a little. I guessed he was wondering about his train. The windows had been cleaned and there was no hearse ahead of us to shower us with dust, but I don't remember anything particular about the sun-gutted countryside. At the España, in the awkward moment or two after we stepped out on to the pavement, she spoke to the German, who looked at his watch and nodded.

"And you, Ty?" Her eyes were leaden.

"I'm sorry. I didn't understand what you said."

"Mister Meinhardt is coming in for a drink. I wondered—"

"Not now, if you don't mind." I'm sure she was glad, though there was no way of telling. "But perhaps you'd dine with me tonight?"

She hesitated momentarily. "Thank you."

"I'll come about seven." I paused. "Is there anything I can do meanwhile?" I said it like something learned by heart.

She shook her head. I gripped the German's sweaty hand, muttered a farewell and left them going up the steps together.

I made my way through the heat to the Bar Sinbad and collected the car, hoping that Joaquin either wasn't on duty or wouldn't see me. There were two things I wanted to do and I drove first to the church. I couldn't find a priest, but a cleaner on her knees in the sanctuary obligingly went and fetched one. He was very young and serious and wore horn-spectacles which somehow gave him the appearance of a comedian's stooge. It was hard to think of him as one who was invested with special powers.

"I want a Mass said." I suppose he was used to people calling him "father".

"At any particular time?" He had a quiet, pleasant voice which he employed slowly and deliberately, as if he were none too sure of my intelligence.

"I doesn't matter in the least. Is there some offering I should make?"

I thought he was weighing me up, about to double the price as they do in the shops when they spot a tourist. But he said: "That is entirely up to you."

I gave him two hundred pesetas: he protested mildly. "It's much too much."

"You could say more than one Mass, perhaps?"

"I could do that, of course." He wrinkled his nose. "What is the name, please?"

"Zavella," I said. "Luis Zavella."

As he wrote it down he remarked: "I seem to know the name."

"It's probably in the morning papers."

"A relative of yours?" His eyesight must have been extra poor.

"An acquaintance."

I started to leave, but he said: "You'll want to know the days; when they can be fitted in."

"I'm not particular."

"But you'll wish to attend, surely?"

"No."

"It is customary."

"Say them when it suits you."

I thanked him and went away, the pigmy gesture made. I have heard it said that only when one is happy can one entirely lose one's identity. But pity can also annihilate selfishness, and hatred can give the illusion of doing so. I walked past the side altars on my way out: the candle-lit gloom gave the same eerie quality to the statuary as in The White Caves. The Saint Christopher, in particular, bore a disturbing resemblance to the stalagmite near the entrance to The Hall of Flags and the sight of it clinched my mood for where I was heading next.

I took the car to the square. A notice outside the main entrance to the Civil Guard building insisted that the space be kept clear, but I parked in front of it and went in. I'd last seen the sergeant who was on duty when Ilsa had called on Romero earlier in the week. He'd stopped me from going beyond the barrier then, and though he tried to do so again I shoved him aside and barged through the pass-gate.

I opened Romero's door without knocking. He was cleaning his finger-nails, lolling back, jacket off, feet resting on the desk. The sergeant lumbered in after me, protesting, apologizing. Curtly, Romero ordered him out of the room. Apart from lifting his head he hadn't moved, but his jaw-muscles knotted, quaking his sallow cheeks.

"This is a surprise, Señor Tyler."

During the Mass and in the cemetery he'd pretended I wasn't there, close though we had sometimes been. Now he had no option, but his mind clearly wasn't on what he imagined was a condescending smile. More than anything he must have begrudged me my secret.

I stopped in front of the desk. "I hope you didn't damage too many stalagmites."

"I'm happy to say not."

"That must have been very gratifying."

"Fortunately it wasn't as difficult as we had feared. He didn't have much ammunition. We switched the lights off until we were through the tunnel, of course. One of my guards was slightly wounded, but that was all."

"Someone must be very proud of you—in addition to yourself."

"I only did my duty, señor."

"That's what Scheele would have claimed."

It was an unguarded retort, but Romero applied his own interpretation and nodded. "What happened yesterday can only be a source of satisfaction to his wife. I took the opportunity of calling on her last night."

"I was certain you would." The broken fan squeaked overhead; endlessly flicked a bar of shadow round the room. "When's his funeral?"

"That is a matter for the Church, not for me."

"You just kill them, is that it?"

"Very rarely." For all his superficial aplomb he was unsure of himself. As if to buttress his uncertainty he said with careful derision: "I keep forgetting Zavella was your friend. In the circumstances, Señora Scheele must find it a most baffling relationship." Encouraged, he added: "However, that won't be why you have come to see me."

"No."

"What do you want then?"

"My passport."

His face clouded. I tossed the receipt he had given me on to the desk. It skidded under the blotter and disappeared, but he didn't attempt to retrieve it. Instead, he made a pretence of studying his finger-nails.

I said impatiently: "You're a bad actor, Romero. I want it now."

"I'm afraid I can't oblige you at the moment."

"No?"

"No."

"Give me one acceptable reason."

"It is locked in a filing-cabinet."

"Then I suggest you open the cabinet up and get it out."

He failed to brazen out my glare. But he said. "My clerk has the keys and today he is off duty." He shrugged unconvincingly. "It is regretted, but there it is. You will have to wait. Come back another time: tomorrow, say."

"*You* carry the keys," I said. "You forget I was here on the night Scheele died and that when your clerk left he handed them to you." A thin, white-metal chain looped from his right hip to right-hand trousers' pocket. "You also forget that you aren't wearing your jacket."

He coloured, but said nothing.

"Quickly, please. I'm in a hurry."

He didn't budge.

"If I don't get it now," I said, "I'll take this whole business right to the top and have you blasted out of that chair for good and all. You had no right to my passport in the first place. I only let you have it that evening because I was sick to death of your pestering. You over-reached yourself then—and you know it. ... Now, perhaps, you'll be good enough to take your feet off the desk and give those nails of yours a rest."

He swallowed, then stood up, supposedly believing that by taking his time he could retain his poise. I watched him sort out the correct key and open the middle drawer of one of the cabinets. The fan's sole surviving blade squeaked round and round, like a dog after its own tail. Romero started fumbling through the exposed rack of files, too slowly for my liking.

I prompted him icily: "Don't tell me you're inefficient on top of everything else. What you're looking for is dark blue, over-printed with gold. And in case it's slipped your mind the name is Tyler."

He produced it sullenly; thudded the drawer back in. Returning, he threw the passport down on the desk in front of me. It hit one corner of the blotter, spinning it, and the receipt was ejected on to the floor at his feet. I said: "Thank you for nothing," then turned on my heels and strode from his office and down the long corridor to the pass-gate and the bright glare of the main door beyond, trembling under the impact of the smallest and most futile of triumphs.

2

Ilsa said: "Captain Romero came to see me last night. Did you know?"

"Yes."

"You were there, he said—at The White Caves."

I nodded. "He asked me to go."

"He told me it was Zavella who asked."

"So it was. But it was Romero who telephoned. That's why I left you in such a hurry."

"You might have explained."

"There wasn't time, Ilsa. He gave me only half an hour to get there."

"Even so you could have said something. It wouldn't have taken a minute."

"I'm sorry."

"You've changed, Ty."

"That's not true."

She shook her head. "You've changed."

We were in the Siroco, a small restaurant which overlooked the south beach. I had taken Ilsa there so as to be on neutral ground: it had no associations for either of us. The Bar Sinbad would have been impossible, and most of the other places where we might have eaten faced northwards towards the Villa Miramar. It was quite dark and, below us, the sea was already black under the ice-blue stars. The tell-tale stain from Gondra still disfiguring the north beach would have been invisible but our wounds were raw enough without deliberately confronting the long arc of sand where we had walked together and where Scheele had floated in.

"In what way have I changed?"

She was silent, telling herself.

Without hope of being believed, I said: "I promise you I haven't."

"You must have been aware of what a terrible thing Zavella had done."

I replied carefully: "Romero didn't inform me until I arrived."

"Afterwards, I mean. Yet you didn't come back. I waited for you, but you didn't come. I can't understand that."

"I'm sorry."

"Why didn't you, Ty?"

She was more bewildered than vindictive. There was no sharpness in her tone: it matched her appearance—weary to the point of exhaustion. Sleep was what she needed.

"I meant to."

She raised her chin incredulously. "It was the same with Erich's ring. You said nothing about that either until it suited you."

"I wanted to get hold of it first—I told you so yesterday."

"And then you said something about the initials not being his."

"I was only making sure there wasn't some mistake."

"How could there have been?" A memory provoked disdain. "You behaved as if ES stood for someone else—as if more than one person had lost an identical ring."

I thought: Don't tempt me, Ilsa. I'm as tired as you are

and can't bear to be hurt any more. And this hurts above all. I love you—that's why I've tied my hands behind my back. So dont molest me too much. Otherwise I'll only start defending myself.

Inshore, ghostly ribs of white moved on the dark sea as though it breathed. Presently, Ilsa said: "What did Zavella want?"

"He hoped I'd deliver a message to a relative of his."

"And will you?" She looked at me as if I were an accessory.

"I'll do my best."

"It's strange that he should have asked for you."

"I suppose he couldn't think of anyone else. I'd met him that morning to get the ring and when he was trapped—"

"What was he like?"

"Small, consumptive. In his early thirties."

"Did he speak about what happened?"

"No."

I gazed out of the window at the lights of some sardine boats. My fingers found the place on the back of my neck, close to the cropped hair, where, four days ago, her nails had torn the skin. The marks had not healed, but the fever which had put them there was as dead as Scheele; had died with him. I had thought that I had lived for her body alone, but I was wrong: there are secret places in the heart to which stress and suffering give existence. Yet, though I had discovered the courage to accept defeat, I lacked stature. She had washed her hands of me: otherwise I wouldn't have held my tongue. If I had believed there was one chance in a thousand of winning her I would have told her everything I knew, filled her mind with all the filth of Gondra, gone without pity and searched for more wherever in Europe it might have been found. But she had finished with me. Scheele hadn't diminished as my vanity had once insisted he would. While he lived we had deceived him, but his death—and the timing of it—had made our deceit profane. I had been rejected in mind and heart; in the confessional and at the communion-rail.

Ilsa said: "You hated Erich, didn't you?"

Once more I remembered Zavella and his plea not to pass the disease on—"It will eat her away from the inside just as it's eaten me away. Why should she suffer, too?" And with anguish I thought: Amen.

"I love you," I answered, looking at her, enormously moved by the symmetry of her small, boyish face, wanting as never before to cup it in my hands: touch her soft, straight hair.

"You only imagined you did—and I am to blame for it."

"Since then. ... Now."

"Please, Ty. I don't want to hear any more."

"All right," I said quietly. "You won't, I promise you. Never again. But I wanted you to know."

Nothing could shake her loyalty. "Only yesterday you were on the point of saying ugly things about Erich. 'He's best forgotten', you said."

I nodded, bitterness seeping in again; drawing the line at an apology.

"That isn't love, Ty," she said. "If you love someone you don't go out of your way to hurt them."

Imprisoned within myself I thought heavily: Why else am I sparing you? Then, because there seemed nothing else to say, I suggested we went in to dinner.

CHAPTER ELEVEN

THE Air France Constellation glittered on the oil-smudged apron and the runways pointed into the quivering distances. On one side were blue hills, their crumpled serrations hazed over with heat; on the other, invisible from the airport's departure block, the sea.

I seemed to have spent the greater part of my time with Ilsa in bars and restaurants and hotel lounges. Since Tuesday evening, in all our crises, we had invariably been besieged by other voices, other moods. Now, for once, I would not have wished it otherwise. I wanted every second peopled with activity; distractions.

"What time d'you reach Paris?"

"About six, I think."

"And you connect straight away?"

"I believe I will have to wait about half an hour."

I had asked her the self-same things on the drive from Bandaques, but one becomes repetitious as the minutes slowly dwindle away, filling each pause with desperate improvisations. Everything had been said that would ever be said, yet silence seemed a crime. Would she like something to read? Was she a good traveller?—or would she be happier with a pill? The very questions underlined how incompletely I knew her: and yet each tired gesture and response twisted in the awakened places of my heart. In seven hours or so she would be in Hamburg, but there was no comfort for me in the myth that the world is shrinking. We were already severed: Scheele's initials had mocked me for the last time when the porter unloaded his three matching travelling cases from the car's boot. There was nothing to be done except wait for the tinny announcement of her flight. The minutes stretched out elastically and I was torn between willing them to an end and staving off the final moment of farewell. But at last the disembodied voice clicked on: "Will passengers for Air France Flight Number 520 for Paris please make their way. ..." And it was as if all the frontier posts everywhere had suddenly come down; like hearing a life sentence delivered.

"Good-bye, Ilsa."

How conventionally we behave in an effort to hide ourselves away: an onlooker might have supposed that we were no more than casually acquainted. But the truth was in our eyes, as frankly and fleetingly exposed as at the instant of our first coming physically together. For the minutest period of time I could have deluded myself that Scheele no longer seemed to be between us.

"Good-bye, Ty." Her hand was cool and she didn't falter. "Try not to think too badly of me."

I was numb; sealed off by the inadequacy of words. "Good-bye. ... Safe and sound"—and the chance phrase gave life to a memory in her mind; in both our minds. I thought she was going to say something more, but she bit her lower lip, regret and disillusion re-possessing her. Like a stranger who'd asked me the way she turned swiftly and, without a backward glance, joined the group of passengers making for the numbered door. I could scarcely believe that I would never see her again or hear that quiet, slightly accented voice. There would be no letters, no telephone-calls. Whether she was going to a house or an apartment, I didn't know. Who would meet her, I didn't know. How she would spend tomorrow—all the tomorrows— I didn't know.

The door flapped to behind her and something inside me shrivelled away to nothing. I must have remained staring at the door for a long time because a girl in a blue uniform came and inquired helpfully whether there was anything I wanted. I heard myself answer, but have no idea what I said that could have made her look at me so strangely. Then I went emptily into the dazzle of the sun and tried to remember where I had left the car.

About thirty miles south of Barcelona I had seen a plane go over; watched it as if it had been Ilsa's. Now, an hour later, the high, slim tower of the Church of the Incarnation pricked the skyline. She would be in Paris by the time I reached the villa.

The numbness had gone deeper. I was like a swimmer who had lost his strength and was being carried unwillingly on the tide. With the resignation of the powerless I told myself again and again that I had been right to allow her to go still believing in Scheele. But it made an unconsoling litany. A sign at a junction pointed towards The White Caves, and Zavella's words about time winning in the end were better suited to my barren mood. Sooner or later we were all losers; we all paid. Scheele had. Zavella had. Ilsa, despite the efficacy of the confessional, imagined she would eventually. And I was paying now, in the desolate sense of loss that Catholics will tell you is their understanding of Hell.

Bandaques gradually hemmed me in. I drove through the town's scabrous streets until, at the amphitheatre, I reached its central hub; then on past the España and the square where Romero's headquarters and the Bar Sinbad faced each other through the plane trees. There was going to be no escape. Gondra had left its livid stain along the beach and as I entered the house, Catalina was singing:

> *Por de bajo del puente*
> *No pasa nadie. ...*

I went into the living-room where Scheele's body had oozed water and Ilsa had come to identify him. She had left no souvenirs. Her wet footprints had long since dried on the tiles; the crumpled bed had long since been smoothed. And yet her presence filled the house—as did Scheele's and

Romero's, as did Zavella's from that other time. Dead or living they had all been here. I walked through on to the terrace and shut the doors against Catalina's singing. The cover on the typewriter was like a flag of defeat. Near the machine was an old copy of *The Oxford Book of Children's Verse* which I had taken out a few days earlier with the intention of giving to Joaquin, but which now I never would. Beside it, weighted down by the cigarette-lighter which had fooled Zavella, was the slip of paper bearing the words: *We are swords that spirits fight with. We never see the hands that brandish us.* ... I screwed it up and tossed it away: the breeze of the sea chased it into the garden. True or false it made no difference.

I lit a cigarette, watching the day die behind the mauve sierras.

I'll have to go away, I thought. I can't stay here. I'll have to go home.

Other Top Notch Thrillers from Ostara Publishing

Brian Callison: *A Flock of Ships*
ISBN 9781906288358
Francis Clifford: *Time is an Ambush*
ISBN 9781906288365
Adam Hall: *The Ninth Directive*
ISBN 9781906288372
Philip Purser: *Night of Glass*
ISBN 9781906288297
Geoffrey Rose: *Clear Road to Archangel*
ISBN 9781906288303
George Sims: *The Terrible Door*
ISBN 9781906288280
Alan Williams: *Snake Water*
ISBN 9781906288310
Alan Williams: *The Tale of the Lazy Dog*
ISBN 9781906288341

All Ostara titles can be ordered from our website
www.ostarapublishing.co.uk **or from your local bookshop**

All titles also available from
Heffers
20 Trinity Street Cambridge CB2 3NG
Telephone 01223 568568
Email literature@heffers.co.uk

Lightning Source UK Ltd.
Milton Keynes UK
UKOW04f0838060514

231179UK00016B/626/P